Knut Hamsun

Hanna Astrup Larsen

Knut Hamsun

ISBN: 978-1-63637-738-4

CONTENTS

The Wanderer

The Poet

The Citizen

THE WANDERER

EARLY LIFE IN NORWAY

Knut Hamsun has become identified in our minds with the lonely figure that recurs again and again in his earlier books, the Wanderer who is for ever outside of organized society and for ever pays the penalty of being different from the crowd and unable to conform to its standards. That this lonely creature is really himself in a certain period of his life we know from the testimony of his own works. Yet this vagabond and iconoclast sprang from the most conservative stock of Norway. He is the descendant of an old peasant family in Gudbrandsdalen, one of the interior mountain valleys in the heart of the country.

Gudbrandsdalen is a region of proud historical traditions. There, nine centuries ago, King Saint Olaf struggled to foist the new religion on a stiff-necked race of pagans, and not far from Hamsun's birthplace one of the oldest churches in Norway proclaimed his victory. There, six centuries ago, the Scotch invader Sinclair was annihilated with all his force when "the peasants of Vaage and Lesje and Lom their whetted axes shouldered," as the ballad tells us, and the story is still cherished,

1

still repeated to every traveller. In this as in other secluded valleys in Norway a peasant aristocracy developed, a hard, strong race, intensely proud of its family and land, looking on any one who had been less than three generations in the neighborhood as an interloper, and scorning the classes of people who were not rooted to the soil by inherited homesteads. For the Norwegian roving blood is strangely tempered by a passionate attachment to inherited land, a trait that is perhaps a salutary safeguard against the national restlessness. Artistic handicrafts flourished in the valley. In the Open Air Museum at Lillehammer we may see them even now, marvellous creations of hammered iron, tapestries picturing scenes from the Bible, wood carvings in mellow colors and with a Renaissance exuberance of design overflowing even the commonest kitchen utensils, all of a rich yet disciplined beauty as if built on age-old artistic traditions and standards.

Hamsun counted among his forefathers many of the artistic craftsmen who set their stamp of culture upon their community. His father's father was a worker in metals. The arts did not bring wealth to those who practised them, however, and his parents at the time of his birth were in straitened circumstances. He was born, August 4, 1859, in Lom, in one of the small well-weathered houses which look so bleak and insignificant against the mighty Gudbrandsdalen uplands. When he was four years old his family removed to the Lofoten Islands, Nordland, in an effort to better their fortunes.

Two strains may be traced in Knut Hamsun's personality. By virtue of his blood and birth he had his roots in a community characterized by an unusually firm and solid culture based on

2

centuries of tradition, and this heritage we shall find coming out in him more and more in his later years. The moralist and preacher who wrote "Growth of the Soil" is a true scion of the best old peasant stock. Through the impressions of his childhood and early youth he became affiliated with the volatile race of Nordland, a people as alien from the heavier inland peasant as if they lived on different continents. The fishermen who play with death for the wealth of the sea and depend for their livelihood on the caprices of nature do not easily harden into traditional moulds. Childish and improvident, witty and sentimental, often fond of the melodramatic, simple and yet shrewd, superstitious but brave beyond all praise, the native of Nordland is a type unlike every other Norwegian. Wherever he may roam, he will yearn for the wonderland of his youth. It is from this Nordland type that Hamsun has created his Wanderer hero, and it was from the nature of Nordland with its alternations of melting loveliness and stark gloom that he drew his poetic inspiration.

At the very time when Hamsun was spending his childhood in the Lofoten Islands, Jonas Lie, the literary discoverer of Arctic Norway, wrote his idyllic little story "Second Sight" in which he has really delineated a "Wanderer" type, his hero being a gifted Nordland lad who is set apart from ordinary people by his strange mental malady and who, wherever he goes, feels himself an alien. In this book, written at a time when not even fixed steamship routes united Nordland with the southern part of the country (railroads are even yet unknown), Jonas Lie has given us a classic description of the country in its virgin state of isolation. It gives the key to that mysterious, extravagant strain which belongs to the Nordland type, and throws light on the sources from which Hamsun drew his hero.

The words that to other people convey only commonplaces become magnified in the Nordland mind accustomed to the ecstatic moods of nature, Lie tells us. Fish to a Nordlanding means Lofoten's and Finmarken's millions, an infinite variety, from the spouting whales that penetrate our fjords driving huge masses of fish like a froth before them, to the tiniest minnow. When he speaks of birds, the Nordlanding does not mean merely an eatable fowl or two, but a heavenly host, billowing in the air like white breakers around the bird crags, shrieking and fluttering and filling the air like a veritable snow-storm over the nesting-places. He thinks of the eider-duck and the tystey; the duck and the sea-pie swimming in fjord and sound or perched on the rocks; the gull, the osprey, and the eagle sailing through the air; the owl moaning weirdly in the mountain clefts—a world of birds. A storm at sea to him means sudden hurricanes that sweep down from the mountains and uproot buildings—so that people at home often have to tie down their houses with chains—waves rushing in from the Arctic Ocean fathoms high, burying big rocks and skerries in their froth and then receding so fast that a ship may be left high and dry and be smashed right in the open sea; hosts of brave men sailing before the wind to save not only their own lives but the dearly bought boatload on which the lives of those at home depend.

"There in the North popular fancy from mythical times has imagined the home of all the powers of evil. There the Lapp has made himself feared by his sorceries, and there at the outermost edge of the world, washed by the breakers of the dark, wintry grey Arctic Ocean, stand the gods of primitive times, the demoniacal, terrible, half formless powers of darkness against

4

whom even the Æsir did battle, but who were not entirely vanquished before St. Olaf with his cruciform sword 'set them in stock and stone.'—The terrors of nature have created an army of evil demons that draw people to them, ghosts of drowned men who have not been buried in Christian earth, mountain titans, the sea draug who sails in his half boat and in the winter nights shrieks terribly out on the fjord. Many a man in real danger has perished because his comrades were afraid of the draug, and we of second sight can see him.

"But even though the overwhelming might of nature bears down with oppressive weight on everything living along that dark, wintry, frothing coast, where nine months of the year are a constant twilight and three of these are without even a glimpse of the sun, so that people's minds become filled with fear of the dark, yet Nordland also possesses the opposite extreme in its sun-warmed, clear-skied, scent-filled summers with their endless play of infinitely varied colors and tints, when distances of seventy or eighty miles seem to melt away so that we can shout across them, when the mountain clothes itself in brownish green grass to the very top—in Lofoten to a height of two thousand feet—and the slender birch trees wreathe the tops of the hills and the edges of the mountain clefts like a dance of sixteen-year-old white-clad girls, while the fragrance of strawberries and raspberries rises to you through the warm air as you pass in your shirt sleeves, and the day is so hot that you long to bathe in the sun-filled, rippling sea which is clear to the very bottom.

"The learned say that the intensities of color and fragrance in the far North are due to the power of the light which fills the air

5

when the sun shines without interruption day and night. Therefore one can not pick so aromatic strawberries and raspberries or so fragrant birch boughs in any other clime. If a fairy idyl has any home, it is certainly in the deep fjord valleys of Nordland in the summer. It is as though the sun were kissing nature so much more tenderly because they have such a short time to be together and must soon part again."

Jonas Lie's description, which I have taken the liberty to quote in abbreviated form, gives a picture of the surroundings in which Hamsun spent his boyhood. It would have been impossible to find any spot in the world more suited to nourish the fancy of an imaginative, impressionable boy. Lonely as he was, he had little to interest him or occupy his mind except what he could find for himself out of doors. He was put to work herding cattle, and spent long dreamy hours alone revelling in the loveliness of the light Nordland summer. It was then he laid the foundation for his habit of roaming alone in the woods and fields, and there he gained that intimate, tender knowledge of nature which appears in his works. In telling of his childhood,

Hamsun says that the animals and birds became his friends. He speaks also of the deep impression which the sea made upon him. His uncle's house, where he spent some of his boyhood, was built above the ocean stream, Glimma, which rushed over a rocky bottom, sometimes one way, sometimes another, according to the tide, but always in motion. Beyond it lay the open sea.

The sharp contrasts of nature, its alternations between darkness and light, are reflected in the temperament of the Nordland

6

people who are easily swung from one extreme to another. Underneath the brightness and levity there is a consciousness of superstitions that are felt sometimes as dark and sinister forces waiting to drag men away from the light into the gloomy void where the evil powers reign. The boy Knut Hamsun's nature was like a sensitive stringed instrument vibrating to the faintest breath of nature's moods, and we find in his works the nervousness, the quick transitions, and the swinging between extremes of exaltation and despair which belong to the Nordland type. While the brightness predominates, the gloom is also present, especially in his earliest, most personal works.

The years he spent with his clergyman uncle were not happy. The uncle had no idea of how to handle a highstrung boy, and his method of education consisted of many lickings, much hard work, and few hours for play. So lonely and dreary was the boy's life that he found his chief amusement in roaming about in the cemetery, spelling out the inscriptions on crosses and slabs, making up stories about them, and talking to himself, or listening to the wind rustling in the grass that grew tall on neglected graves. Occasionally the old weather vane on the church steeple would let out a terrible shriek when the wind veered. It sounded like "iron gritting its teeth against some other iron." Sometimes he would help the old grave-digger in his work, and he had strict injunctions on what to do if bits of bone or tufts of hair worked their way out to the surface. They were to be put back in place and decently covered. Once, however, he ventured to disobey the gravedigger and take with him a tooth which he thought he could use for some little object he was fashioning. In the short story "A Ghost" in the collection "Things that Have Happened to Me," where he draws this dismal story of his childhood, he tells how the dead owner appeared to him and threatened him at intervals for years afterwards, even after he had left the house of his uncle and was living with his parents, where he shared a room with his brothers and sisters. The apparition froze him with fear and tortured him so that he was often tempted to throw himself in the Glimma and end it all. Of the effect that this incident had upon him he writes: "This man, this red-bearded messenger from the land of death, did me much harm by the unspeakable gloom he cast over my childhood. Since then I have had more than one vision, more than one strange encounter with the inexplicable but nothing that has gripped me with such force. And yet perhaps the effect upon me was not all harmful. I have often thought of that. It has occurred to me that he was one of the first things that made me grit my teeth and harden myself. In my later experiences I have often had need of it."

In view of the high position clergymen hold in Norway, and especially considering the prestige attached to the official class fifty years ago, it seems odd that a clergyman's nephew, an inmate of his house for years, should have been slated for a shoemaker, but evidently there was no money with which to send Knut to school, and perhaps his mental gifts were not of the caliber to promise that he would fit easily into any one of the usual professional niches. After his confirmation, which is the Norwegian boy's entrance to manhood, he was therefore apprenticed to a cobbler in the city of Bodö on the mainland. In his own mind, however, he was quite determined that he was to be a poet, and it was while working for the cobbler that he published his first literary venture, a highly romantic poem called "Meeting Again." This was followed by the story "Björger, by Knud Pedersen Hamsund," a gloomy, introspective tale of an orphaned peasant boy and a lady of high degree who died for love of him—a foreshadowing of the motif in "Victoria." In spite of its immaturity, its absurdity even, the story, according to the judgment of critics to-day, shows flashes of Hamsun's peculiar genius. Alas, there were no critics wise and sympathetic enough to see its promise at the time, if indeed any critics read it. The book was printed by the nineteen-year-old author at his own expense, paid for by his hard-earned savings, and was bought by a few people in Bodö, but hardly circulated beyond the confines of the city.

Naturally the cobbler's bench could not long confine his restlessness, and, after a short experience as a coal-heaver on the docks of Bodö—where his eye-glasses attracted amused attention as out of keeping with his work—Hamsun set out on the wanderings that were to last full ten years. He taught a little school, was clerk in a sheriff's office, and crushed stones on the road.

The experiences of this period were the foundation of his two novels "Under the Autumn Star" and "A Wanderer Plays with Muted Strings," bound in the English edition under the common title "Wanderers." Written many years later from the standpoint of an elderly citizen who leaves his home in the city to revisit the haunts of his youth and play at being a vagrant laborer once more, they give his adventures in the softening light of retrospect. A touch of personal description may be found in the lines, "I taught myself to walk with long, tenacious steps. The proletarian appearance I had already in my face and hands."

There is a lingering tenderness in the author's treatment of these years which would indicate that at the time of writing he looked back upon them almost with regretful longing. We do not find the smallest trace of the acrid bitterness which he put into the short stories from his American experiences or into the account of his struggles to gain a foothold in Christiania. The roving life without fixed habitation or routine had its charms for him and it gave him an opportunity to be much out of doors. Strong and capable as he was, the manual labor in itself held no terrors for him, and he was rather proud of his inventive skill. "Under the Autumn Star" recounts a number of small technical triumphs, chief among which was a marvellous saw for cutting timber on the root—an actual invention of Hamsun's. Not many years ago he replied in answer to a question in an enquête that the proudest achievement of his life was the invention of this saw, in the practicability of which he still had faith, although I believe it has never been perfected for actual use.

During the time when he ate and slept with servants and tramped the road with other day laborers, while observing the upper class from the vantage point of his own obscurity, Hamsun garnered a full sheaf of those curious and startling incidents by means of which he keeps his readers in a constant state of surprise. Meanwhile he did not forget his old ambition to become a poet. He felt the need of an education, and gradually worked his way southward to Christiania, where he entered the University.

The experiment was not a success. At that time the University was much more than now under the influence of old academic traditions, and did not welcome the rustic in search of knowledge as cordially as perhaps it would have done to-day. Moreover, the former cobbler and road-laborer was uncouth in his manner, bursting with loud-voiced opinions, and by no means filled with the proper reverence for authority. He soon realized that he was a misfit in University circles, and gave up the attempt in disgust. Of more benefit to him was a trip to the continent which he was enabled to make. After his return he went back to his old life on the road, but his intellect was more and more reaching out beyond the humble work by which he earned his living. Finally he made his escape and took passage to America.

FROM THE WHEATFIELDS TO THE FISHING BANKS

In the early eighties, when Hamsun started out for America, the tide of Norwegian immigration was at its height. Not only were thousands and thousands of young men and women going across the sea to try to better their worldly status, but America had come to be looked upon as a spiritual as well as an economic land of promise. The poets, Björnson, Ibsen, Kielland, Jonas Lie and others were busy sending their heroes and heroines over there to find expansion of life or perhaps to come back and be the fresh, salty stream in the back waters of Norwegian narrowness and prejudice. We need only call to mind Lona Hessel in "Pillars of Society." Knut Hamsun had, of course, read these books, and when he started out for the New World he did not go merely as an immigrant to seek his fortune.

He hoped to find those larger opportunities for leading his own life and using his gifts which the poets had been telling him about. He had bruised himself on Old World littleness; quite naturally he looked to the New World for bigger visions, ampler spaces, and a saner estimate of a man's worth. In this he was destined to be sorely disappointed. And yet some of the things he sought, and even more those he learned to value later in life, were there, but he failed to find them.

His dream of being a poet was still alive in him, and when he came to his countrymen in the Middle West he announced to a friend that he was going to write poetry for the Norwegian people in America. To one who knows the Middle Western settlements, there is something pathetic in this youthful ambition. God knows that if any one needs a poet it is the immigrant who is torn violently from his contact with the spiritual life of the old country and has not yet taken root in the new, but the Hamsun of that day had no message which his emigrated countrymen cared to hear. Like other immigrants they were absorbed in the task of building a new community, and when this work left them any leisure they preferred to sing the old songs and dream the old dreams of the fjælls and fjords. Immigrants are generally very conservative, and cling with all the fibres of their affection to the old melodies. They have little ear for any new voice that lifts itself among them. But the Middle West has never at any time had much use for the dreamer and visionary, and in Hamsun's day it was more than now a country of absorption in material things by as much as it was nearer pioneer times.

Hamsun soon found that in order to make his living he would have to work hard under conditions more distasteful to him than his old roving life in Norway. For a while he cherished a hope that he might be able to make his way in some manner more suited to his mental equipment. He came under the influence of a Norwegian writer and clergyman, Kristoffer Janson, of

Minneapolis, who tried to make a Unitarian minister of him. But the faith that tries to modernize religion by eliminating its mystery could not long hold the imagination of one who sees mystery as the very life and essence of religion. In the diatribes on American intellectual life published after his return to Norway he paid his respects to Unitarianism in an essay on Emerson. He cared little for the Concord philosopher. Of the American poets he "could bear to read" certain parts of Walt Whitman, Poe, and Hawthorne, while he referred to our most beloved poet as "the somnolent Longfellow." In Minneapolis he tried to express his unflattering views on American literature in lectures, and hired Dania Hall for the purpose, but Americans of Scandinavian extraction are extremely quick to resent any attack on their adopted country, and refused to listen to him.

When we remember how sober and well draped was the verse of our great New England poets, we can hardly wonder that it failed to satisfy the young author who, a few years later, was to lay bare every quivering nerve of his being in "Hunger." Nor can we wonder that a young immigrant, forced to work hard in rough surroundings, should not have discovered the finest flowers of American culture. It is more remarkable that he who was destined to write the great epic of the pioneer farmer in "Growth of the Soil" should have failed utterly to see the real elemental soundness and vigor of the pioneer community in which he found himself, and that he should never have had his eyes opened to the many obscure Isaks toiling on Norwegian farms in the Middle West. Yet this too can easily be understood when we remember how he thirsted for the richer, subtler life of an old community and how little his thirst had yet been satisfied.

In his later books Hamsun has glorified any kind of work that has to do with practical realities and is done with a will. In his youth he learned by his own experience the deadening, brutalizing effect of toiling under the lash. He was initiated on the wheatfields of North Dakota, where production was carried on with swarms of day laborers. In the winter, on the grip of a Chicago street car, he suffered the hardships of long hours and low pay for uncongenial work. Finally he plumbed the lowest depths he was fated to know when he spent some miserable seasons on a fishing-smack off New Foundland.

Reminiscences of these years are found in a few short stories and sketches scattered through various volumes of his works. "Woman's Victory" a story in "Struggling Life" (1905) is based on his experiences in Chicago, and is prefaced by a paragraph which gives a vivid picture of this phase of his American adventures. It begins: "I was a street car conductor in Chicago. First I had a job on the Halstead line, which was a horse car line running from the centre of town to the cattle market. We who had night duty were not very safe, for there were many suspicious characters passing that way at night. We were not allowed to shoot and kill people, for then the company would have had to pay compensation. However, one is seldom wholly devoid of weapons, and there was the handle of the brake which could be torn off and was a great comfort. Not that I ever had need of it except once.

"In 1886 I stood on my car every night through the Christmas holidays, and nothing happened. Once there came a big crowd of Irishmen out of the cattle market and quite filled my car. They were drunk and had bottles along. They sang loudly and did not

15

seem inclined to pay, although the car started. Now they had paid the company five cents every evening and every morning for another year, they said, and this was Christmas, and they were not going to pay. There was nothing unreasonable in this point of view, but I did not dare to let them off for fear of the company's 'spies' who were on the watch for lapses on the part of conductors. A policeman boarded the car. He stood there for a few minutes, said something about Christmas and the weather, and jumped off again when he saw how crowded the car was. I knew very well that at a word from the policeman all the passengers would have had to pay their fares, but I said nothing. 'Why didn't you report us?' asked one of the men. 'I thought it unnecessary,' said I, 'I am dealing with gentlemen.' At that there were some of them who began to laugh, but others thought I had spoken well, and they saw to it that everybody paid."

The author's North Dakota experiences are the subject of several short stories. "Zacchæus" in the collection "Brushwood" (1903) gives a vivid picture of life on Billibony farm, where work began at three in the morning and went on at a nerve-racking speed until the stars came out at night, and the only comic relief was the serving up to Zacchæus of his own finger in the stew. Yet Zacchæus who treasured this severed member of himself, and the cook who played the gruesome trick because Zacchæus had laid hands on his sacred "library" consisting of one old newspaper and a book of war songs, these were human compared to the creatures described in the sketch "On the Banks" in "Siesta" (1897). Never before or since has Hamsun drawn a picture of such stark and unrelieved hideousness as this description of eight men who were herded together on the boat regardless of race or color, whose chief pleasure was maltreating the fish they caught, and whose obscene talk and lewd dreams rise from the crowded forecastle like a loathsome stench. To the man of nerves and imagination who tells the story, the horror of the situation was deepened by the consciousness of the hostile powers of nature lying in wait out there on the sea which closed around him everywhere and of the unseen monsters in the deep trying to hold what is their own while the men tug frantically at the nets. This sense of being surrounded by hostile forces is very unusual with Hamsun, who generally loves to dwell on the friendliness of nature.

With these months on the fishing banks, the cup was full. Hamsun made up his mind that his wanderings must end and his real work begin, no matter at what cost. He took passage home on a Danish steamer, and came to Christiania in 1888, determined to make his way by writing. He was not wholly unknown in the editorial offices of the city. He had been back in Norway between the years 1883 and 1886, when he had attempted to give lectures on literature, though not with much more success than that which attended his efforts in Minneapolis. During his second sojourn in the United States he had written some correspondences to Norwegian papers.

Before beginning his serious literary work, Hamsun threw off at white heat a book entitled "Intellectual Life in Modern America" (1889). It is full of prejudice and misinformation: arraignment of American culture after following resplendently attired servant girls on the street and listening to their conversation (just as Kipling did); moralizings about the divorce evil based on the stories in sensational newspapers without the slightest knowledge of good American home-life; condemnation of our art museums and opera houses as temples of Mammon, and much more of the same kind. Yet the scathing satire of the book, though biased, does not always miss its mark. Hamsun's shrewdness had penetrated to the weakness of American civilization, its externalism, its materialism, its dryness and shallowness. We may also admit that his American experiences fell in a period of little intellectual vitality, when the great New Englanders had been relegated to school declamations, and the modern quickening of liberal thought was yet far distant.

One thing, at least, must be set down to Hamsun's credit. He did not, like many lesser writers from across the sea, fall into the cheap and easy task of ridiculing the simple people of the frontier or making fun of his own countrymen in their uncouth efforts to Americanize themselves. His shafts were always aimed at that which passes for the highest in American civilization. Here as in his later onslaughts on Ibsen and Tolstoy, his audacities loved a shining mark.

There are only a few scattered references in the book to the Norwegian immigrants in this country, and these are full of sympathetic comprehension of their difficulties. This fact, however, has not prevented "Intellectual Life in Modern America" from being a stumbling block and an offense to Americans of Norwegian extraction. It has been one of the main factors in preventing for many years the recognition of his genius among them.

In this connection I recollect the first and only time I have seen Knut Hamsun. It was in 1896, on my first visit to Norway, when

I met him at the home of my relatives, and I can well remember how my own youthful prairie patriotism resented his attacks on the country my parents had made their own. As I think of him at this distance of years, with tolerance for his views on America, with charity for other things not acceptable to the staid household of which I was a member, I remember him as a man of distinguished presence, still in the flush of young manhood. He was distinctly of the fair, virile type met in the eastern mountain districts where he was born, tall, broad-shouldered, with a particularly fine profile and well-shaped head which he carried in a regal manner. He was then at the height of his early fame.

THE AUTHOR OF "HUNGER"

Knut Hamsun, like more than one other Norwegian genius, won his first recognition in Denmark, where he spent a few months after his return from the United States. Edvard Brandes, at that time editor of the Copenhagen daily "Politiken," has told a story of a young Norwegian who one day presented himself at the office with a manuscript. The editor was about to refuse it on the ground of unsuitable length, when something in the appearance of the stranger made the refusal die on his lips. It was the shabbiest, most emaciated figure that had ever crossed the editorial threshold, but there was something in the pale, trembling face and the eyes behind the glasses that moved the editor in spite of himself. He took the manuscript home with him and began to read it. As he read the story of the starving young genius, it dawned on him with a sense of shame that the writer was probably at that moment without the means of subsistence. Hastily he enclosed a ten krone bill in an envelope, addressed it to the place the unknown author had given as his residence, and ran to the station to mail it. Then he returned and read on to the last paragraphs, where the hero is stealthily crawling up to his room, afraid to rouse a wrathful landlady, and is moved to a delirium of joy by the receipt of a letter containing a ten krone bill sent him by an editor—ten kroner being the highest pitch of opulence to which Hamsun ever carries his hero.

In telling the coincidence that same evening to a Swedish critic, Axel Lundegård, who has published the story, Brandes spoke of how the manuscript had impressed him. "It was not only that it showed talent. It somehow caught one by the throat. There was about it something of a Dostoievsky."

"Was it really so remarkable?" asked Lundegård. "What was the title of it?"

"Hunger."

"And the author?"

"Knut Hamsun."

"It was the first time I heard the name Knut Hamsun," writes Lundegård, "and the first time I heard the phrase 'something of a Dostoievsky' used about any of his books. Since then it has become a commonplace, but applied to the first production of a young author by a critic not at all given to over-enthusiasm, it was a tribute."

Through the influence of Edvard Brandes the manuscript, which contained the first chapters of the book "Hunger," was placed with a new radical Copenhagen magazine, "New Soil." This was in 1888. The story was anonymous, but it attracted attention by its exotic brilliance of style and by the intensity which up to that time had been unknown in Northern literature. Rumors of its authorship were current, and were confirmed when, in 1890, the book "Hunger" burst upon a startled Christiania and made its author instantly famous.

In the intervening time Hamsun had gained some notoriety in his own country by the publication of "Intellectual Life in Modern America." Although he had thus trumpeted forth his failure to find any stirring of the intellect whatever in the great American republic, the Norwegian critic Sigurd Hoel attributes the style of "Hunger" to American influence. It had a daredevil humor, a dash and verve, and a feeling for effect that certainly had no precedent in the respectable annals of Norwegian literature.

"It was the time when I went about and starved in Christiania, that strange city which no one leaves before it has set its mark upon him,"—so runs the oft-quoted first sentence in "Hunger." There is no reason why it should have been Christiania. It might as well have been the American brain market, New York, or any other city where men and women try to sell the product of their brains and learn that their finest thoughts and highest efforts are not of the slightest consequence to anybody. Hundreds of men and women have fought the fight to which he has given classic expression. They will recognize his astonishment as it dawned upon him that although he had "the best brain in the country and shoulders that could stop a truck," there was no place for him in the great machine that ground food for the dullest and stupidest. They will know the bending of the neck and the sagging of the spirit, the hysterical swinging between absurd pride and shameless grasping at any opportunity, the agonized

22

striving to catch the eye and ear of an indifferent world by strained and overwrought work, the impotent sense of never being able to begin the fight on equal terms.

Few, however, have dared to follow the experiment to the uttermost ends of destitution. Few have explored the abysses of suffering through which Hamsun leads his hero. At one time he tried to bully a poor frightened cashier into stealing five öre (a little over a cent) from the cash drawer so that he could buy bread with it. Another time he refused the offer of an editor to pay him in advance for an article not yet written. Once he suddenly decided to beg the price of a little food from some big business man whose name had suddenly come into his head with the force of an inspiration, and persisted, humiliating himself to the depths, holding his ground till he was practically thrown out. Another time, when he himself had starved for days, he pawned his vest to get a krone to give a beggar. It is just such absurdities and inconsistencies that people commit when the starch of everyday habits has been washed out of them.

He keeps back nothing in his story. He even relates with grim humor an encounter with a girl of the streets who in pity offers to take him home with her although he has no money, while he simulates virtue to conceal his abject state: "I am Pastor So-and-so. Go away and sin no more." But his realism does not consist merely in dragging out into the light the acts that others commit in the dark. One need not be a genius to do that. No, he plumbs below action, below even conscious thought and feeling, to those erratic impulses that would make criminals or maniacs of us all if we followed them, not only the great overmastering passions that have their place in the Decalogue, but all the fitful whims

23

and inconsequential trifles that influence conduct. It is as though the delirium of hunger had released all that which is usually controlled by will or custom. Sometimes, when he has starved for days, he can feel his brain as it were detaching itself from the rest of his personality, going its own way, manufacturing idiotic conceits, which he knows to be idiotic, but can not stop. Yet all the time his other consciousness is sitting by, holding the pulse of his delirious imagination and recording its antics.

The light, whimsical touch rarely fails him, but occasionally there are passages of a sombre and thrilling pathos, as the following: "God had thrust His finger down into the tissue of my nerves and gently, quite casually, disarranged the fibres a little. And God had drawn His finger back, and behold, there were shreds and fine root filaments on His fingers from the tissue of my nerves. And there was an open hole after the finger which was God's finger and wounds in my brain where His finger had passed. But when God had touched me with the finger of His hand, he left me alone and did not touch me any more."

Once he cursed God. He had begged a bone of a butcher under pretense of giving it to his dog, and hid it under his coat until he came to a doorway where he could take it out and gnaw it. But the noxious bits came up again as fast as he could swallow them, while the tears streamed from his eyes, and his whole body shook with nausea. Then he screamed out his imprecations: "I tell you, you sacred Ba'al of heaven, you do not exist, but if you did I would curse you so that your heaven should tremble with the fires of hell. I tell you, I have offered you my service, and you have refused it, and I turn my back on you forever, because you did not know the time of your visitation. I tell you that I know I am going to die, and yet I scorn you, you heavenly Apis, in the teeth of death. You have used your power over me, although you know that I never bend in adversity. Ought you not to know it? Did you form my heart in your sleep? I tell you, my whole life and every drop of blood in me rejoices in scorning you and spitting on your grace. From this moment I renounce you and all your works and all your ways; I will curse my thought if it thinks of you and tear off my lips if they ever again speak your name. I say to you, if you exist, the last word in life or in death — I say farewell." But the imp of irony, which in Hamsun is never far away, is peeping over his shoulder as he writes, and the blasphemies are hardly cold on the page before he tells himself that they are "literature." He is conscious of forming his curses so that they read well. This outburst stands alone in his works. It is as though in "Hunger" he had once for all rid himself of all the accumulated rage and agony of his youth. They never come again.

The book is without beginning and end and without a plot, but it has a series of climaxes. Each section describes some phase of hunger and its attendant sufferings: the physical deterioration and weakness, the rebellion of spirit, the hallucinations, the shame and degradation. When the strain becomes intolerable, the tension suddenly snaps with the receipt of five or ten kroner, and then Hamsun instantly removes his hero from our sight. We never see him in the enjoyment of this comparative opulence, but when the money is gone, we meet him again beginning the old struggle, though each time weaker and more unfit to take up the fight. He never achieves anything; his small successes in occasionally selling a manuscript never lead to anything. The book is a record of defeat and frustration which have at last become inevitable because something in himself has given way. Even his strange love affair with the girl whom he calls Ylajali ends in baffled disappointment.

Finally Hamsun simply cuts the thread of the story by letting his hero ship as an ordinary seaman in a boat that is going to England. He leaves the city he had set out to conquer. The city has conquered him. "Out in the fjord I straightened up once and, drenched with fever and weakness, looked in toward land and said good-bye for this time to the city of Christiania, where the windows shone so brightly in all the homes."

THE POET

HIS OWN HERO

The most adequate idea of Hamsun's artistic personality can be gained by reading his early works from "Hunger" to "Munken Vendt" and preferably reading them in the order of their appearance.

Through the medley of characters there emerges a distinct type that can be traced in one after the other of his early books but disappears in the later, more objective, pictures of whole communities. This person is at first always the hero in whom everything centres; later he steps into the background as an onlooker who is sometimes the author's spokesman. He is always a dreamer and one who stands outside of organized society; but this aloofness is not self-sought. On the contrary, he often suffers in his loneliness, and is longing and struggling to come within the circle of human fellowship, but there is something in his own nature which unfits him to be a cog in the common machinery. His pulses are differently attuned from those of other people. The standards by which happiness and success are usually measured mean nothing to him, but he can be lifted to exaltation by the fragrance of a flower or the humming of an insect. He is often a poet, if not in actual production at least in his temperament, and has the poet's responsiveness to things that more thick-skinned people do not notice. An ugly face, a jarring noise can shiver his highest mood like crystal and plunge him to the depths of despair. A sour look or an unkind word or even a trifling mishap—the loss of a lead pencil when he is inspired to write—can cast a gloom over his day. He is full of generous impulses which sometimes take erratic forms and is capable of carrying self-sacrifice to the most senseless extreme, but his nature has never a drop of meanness. He revels in communing with nature and finds pleasure in the society of some lowly friend or simple, loving woman, but any happiness that life may bring him is never more than a momentary gleam. He never lives to his full potentiality either in achievement or in passion. The Swedish critic John Landquist puts the question why we never tire of this oft-repeated Hamsun hero any more than of his Swedish cousin Gösta Berling, and answers that it is because he never gains anything and never turns any situation to his own advantage.

There is no doubt that this constantly recurring figure is Hamsun himself in one incarnation after another. He has pointed the connection by personal description, by reference to his authorship, and once even by the use of his own name. He has to a greater extent than most creative artists drawn for his subjects on his own varied experiences, and though he has of course transmuted them in his imagination, it is clear that he has at least been near enough to the events he records to have lived through them very intensely in his own mind. This is, of course, notably true of "Hunger," which was written at the age of thirty, when his own experiences as a journalistic free lance in Christiania were still fresh in his mind. It is true also of "Mysteries," "Pan," and "Victoria," each one of which corresponds to some phase in his own development. In "Munken Vendt" and "Wanderers" there are reminiscences from his vagabond days, and it is significant of the subjectivity with which he enters into the person of his hero that in the latter he has chosen to make the narrator a man of his own age at the time of writing rather than reincarnate himself in the image of his youth. In the earlier books, on the other hand, the hero is always young, generally between twenty-five and thirty.

The Hamsun ego as the critic of contemporary phenomena, the outsider who is unable to fit himself into any clique or party, appears in Höibro of "Editor Lynge," who is carried over into the drama "Sunset," and in Coldevin of "Shallow Soil." He is absent from all the author's later, more objective, novels, "Dreamers," "Benoni," "Rosa," "Children of the Age," "Segelfoss City," and "Women at the Pump," but we may perhaps find a shadow of him in Sheriff Geissler of "Growth of the Soil," the garrulous wiseacre who "knew what was right, but did not do it."

The typical traits of the young Hamsun hero are found in the highest degree in Johan Nagel. The central figure of "Mysteries" (1892) is a reincarnation of the nameless narrator of "Hunger," a few years older, gentler, but no less erratic, and even more sensitive. There is about him a great lassitude, an indifference to his own advancement in life, which might easily be the aftermath of great suffering and terrible struggles. He seems to have no purpose of any kind. He steps ashore one day in a small Norwegian seacoast town simply because it looks so pleasant to a returned wanderer, and there he remains, startling the inhabitants by his odd manners and freakish garments. There is an exquisite goodness in Nagel. His attitude is no longer that of the clenched fist. He tries to win his way into the fellowship of his neighbors by acts of quixotic generosity—which another impulse leads him to cover up. He takes infinite pains to find opportunities of giving pleasure to the outcasts of the community without letting them know whence the bounty comes. He loves to decoy a beggar into a doorway and bestow a large sum upon him with strict injunctions to secrecy. He has in the highest degree the sweetness and longing for affection which is a leading trait in all the Hamsun heroes, though least apparent in the youngest of them, the narrator of "Hunger;" but he has also in a superlative degree their unfitness for the common affairs of men. Consequently he suffers the fate of those who would do good as it were from the outside without being a part of the community for which they would sacrifice themselves: his efforts fall fruitless to the ground.

Into this book Hamsun has introduced a curious parody of the hero, a little wizened cripple who is like a deformed reflection of Nagel. This poor devil carries goodness, meekness, and long-suffering to a point where it merely rouses the beast in the respectable citizens of the small town and draws on himself brutal persecution; but underneath his real goodness there is some abyss of evil which we are not allowed to fathom, but which Nagel understands by a strange intuition. His efforts to warn and save his protegé are unavailing. Unsuccessful too are

30

his efforts to win the confidence of Martha Gude to whom he turns for consolation when Dagny rejects his love. Nagel is an artist nature, and in the latter part of the book he is revealed as a violinist with at least a touch of real genius, but he has been thoroughly disillusioned regarding himself and his art. He will not be one of the swarm of little geniuses or cater to the beef-eaters. Whatever possibilities of achievement still lie dormant in him are completely destroyed by his unhappy love affair.

Written at a time when Hamsun from the lecture platform was carrying on a campaign against the older poets and the established literary standards, "Mysteries" is made the vehicle of many iconoclastic opinions, and Nagel is to a greater extent than most of his heroes made the mouthpiece of the author's views. In long rambling talks, sometimes carried on with himself as sole audience, he attacks Ibsen, Tolstoy, Gladstone, and other great names of the day. In the books immediately following "Mysteries," "Editor Lynge" and "Shallow Soil," Hamsun continues his attacks on the ideals of the day, though in them he directs his blows rather at the small imitators of the great.

The Hamsun hero in his relation to nature appears in "Pan" (1894). Lieutenant Glahn, the central figure of the book, is a hunter who has lived in the forest until he has himself taken on something of the nature of an animal in the look of his eyes and in his manner of moving. He is supremely happy in his hut. His senses are saturated with the warmth of summer days, the fragrance of roots and trees, the soughing of the woods, and the tiny noises of all the things that live in the forest. His spirit rests in the sense that in nature all things go on, tiny streamlets trickle their melodies against the mountainside though no one hears them, the brook rushes to the ocean, and everything is renewed each year regardless of human fates. With the outdoor life comes the primitive love of shelter which we lose in cities; a warm sense of home ripples through his whole being when he returns to his but in the evening, and he talks to his dog about how comfortable they are.

Glahn has found peace in the forest, but this peace is shattered as soon as he comes in contact with his fellowmen. Awkward and uncouth, he is unable to comport himself with dignity even in the little group of merchants and professional men that constitute society in a Nordland fishing village. He is too proud and simple to cope with the caprices of the woman he has fallen in love with, and she soon tires of him. Then Glahn, moved by a childish desire to make her feel his existence even though it be only by a big noise, arranges a rock explosion, and this foolish feat accidently kills the only person who really loves him, the simple woman whom he has met in the forest. Against his misery now nature, which a few weeks earlier was all in all to him, has no remedy.

Between the appearance of "Pan" and "Victoria" (1898) lay a period of productive work resulting in the publication of the dramatic trilogy centering in the philosopher Kareno and a volume of short stories entitled "Siesta." The increasing success of Hamsun's own authorship set its stamp on the next incarnation of his hero, Johannes, the miller's son in "Victoria" who becomes a poet. Johannes is the only one of all his youthful heroes who is fundamentally a harmonious nature and the only one who masters life. The opening paragraph of the book is like a happier reflection of Hamsun's own dreamy, lonely boyhood.

"The miller's son went around and thought. He was a big fellow of fourteen years, brown from sun and wind and full of ideas. When he was grown up he was going to be a match manufacturer. That was so deliciously dangerous, he might get sulphur on his fingers so that no one would dare to shake hands with him. He would be very much respected by the other boys because of his dangerous trade." Johannes knows all the birds and is like "a little father" to the trees, lifting up their branches when they are weighed down by snow. He preaches to a congregation of boulders in the old granite quarry, and stands dreaming over the mill dam, following the course of the bubbles as they burst in foam. "When he was grown up he was going to be a diver, that's what he was going to be. Then he would step down into the ocean from the deck of a ship and enter strange kingdoms and lands where marvellous forests were waving, and a castle of coral stood on the bottom. And the princess beckons to him from a window and says, 'Come in!'"

Just as Hamsun's own dreams are echoed in this boyish imagery, so his own authorship in its happiest time when he felt all his powers in full swing, is reflected in the later story of Johannes. Between the rude hunter of "Pan" and the poet of "Victoria" there is a lifetime of development. Johannes is just as impulsive and irrepressible as the other Hamsun heroes he is quite likely to burst into loud song in the middle of the night and disturb the neighbors, if a happy idea strikes him, but he has really found himself in his work. Johannes is loved by the young lady of the manor with a love that is strong enough for death, but not strong enough for life. He loses her, but the loss does not blight his life. The great emotion she has given him remains with him to deepen and enrich his nature and to become the life-sap of his blossoming genius.

Very different from the miller's son and yet of the same family is the happy-go-lucky swain who gives his name to the dramatic poem "Munken Vendt" (1902). It is to some degree reminiscent of "Peer Gynt" both in the verse form and in the chief character; but while Ibsen wrote a bloody satire of the worst qualities in his race, Hamsun has drawn a lovable vagabond. Munken Vendt is a student and hunter whose adventures take place in some Norwegian valley at a period not definitely fixed, but certainly much more romantic than the present. He is something of a poet, is clever but unable to turn his gifts to his own advantage, is clothed in rags but always with a feather in his cap and ready to give away his last shirt, wins sweethearts wherever he goes but fails the woman who should have been his mate, and finally throws away his life in a senseless extravagance of self-sacrifice. There is about Munken Vendt, for all his foolishness, a proud defiance of suffering, a noble pathos, a bigness and elevation of thought, which give his portrait a distinctive place in the Hamsun gallery.

The books I have mentioned here are generally regarded as the most individualistic of Hamsun's works and as those that reveal his personality most intimately. Among them should be counted also "The Wild Chorus" (1904), a slender volume of poems which, with "Munken Vendt," constitute all that he has written in metrical form. While Hamsun is most at home in poetic prose, his poems have a wild, fresh charm and are intensely personal expressions of his views on the two subjects that engage him most deeply: love between man and woman and love of nature.

THE HERO AND THE HEROINE

A veritable Shakespearean gallery of women, drawn with subtle insight and delicate sympathy, is found in Hamsun's works. Though infinitely varied in their personalities, they move within certain limits and have certain traits in common. They are intensely feminine with the nervous fitfulness and spasmodic capriciousness that go with overwrought sexual sensibilities. Occasionally he carries a woman through this phase in her life into a warm and passionate motherliness, but never into a finer and more complex individual development. All his heroines have in the highest degree the unfathomable lure of sex, but what they are above and beyond this we never learn.

The limitation may be less in the heroines themselves than in the medium through which we are allowed to see them. If it were possible to mention in the same breath two such antipodes as Jane Austen and Knut Hamsun, I might recall what has been said of her that she never attempts to tell us how men talk when they are away from the presence of women. He never describes a woman when she is alone. We are never allowed to be present when his heroines commune with their own thoughts; we never see them from their own point of view and but rarely from that of a mere observer. We glimpse only so much of them as they reveal to their lovers, and while in this way they never lose the glamour and mystery with which they are surrounded, it is inevitable that they will seem members of a common sisterhood, inasmuch as their lover, the Hamsun hero, is always the same.

In the character of Edvarda in "Pan" the qualities of the Hamsun heroine are heavily underscored. She is a wayward girl with erotic instincts early awakened and with a flighty imagination which sets her lovers absurd tasks, and yet there is a certain sweetness and a primitive freshness about her that attract in spite of better judgment. Her curiosity is roused by Glahn, the hunter with the "eyes like an animal's"; she invites him to her father's house and draws him into their social circle. At a picnic she suddenly flies at him and kisses him in the presence of the assembled village, and after this outburst she meets him constantly, circles around his hut by night, and kisses his very footprints. But in a few days her violence has exhausted itself; she stays away from their trysts; she insults and ridicules him in her own home as publicly as she has formerly favored him, and before many weeks have passed, she has engaged herself to another man. Yet her love for Glahn is real, and presently she makes frantic attempts to get him back. Glahn's stubborn resistance is the measure of the suffering she has inflicted upon him, and when at last she begs him to leave his dog Æsop with her when he departs, he shoots his four-footed friend and sends her the body. He seeks consolation with other women, and there is much sweetness in his relation with Eva, the simple daughter of the people, but in spite of her humble, unquestioning devotion and his real tenderness for her, his feeling never touches the heights or the depths. Even when he is with her, the thought of Edvarda is like a constantly smarting wound. Yet he continues to resist Edvarda's advances. When after the lapse of some years she tries to call him back, he pretends to himself that he does not care, but he goes away to the Indian jungle and seeks death.

Edvarda reappears in a subsequent novel "Rosa," a torn and lacerated soul, forever unsatisfied, with strange gleams of generosity alternating with petty cruelty. She owns that there have been some moments in life not so bad as others, and chief among these to her was the time when she was in love with the strange hunter. In her desperate longing for something that will take her out of herself, she has spasms of religion, but at last sinks to the level of having an erotic adventure with a Lapp in the forest and worshipping his hideous little stone god.

A repellent creature in many ways is Edvarda, and yet the author has managed to make us feel her through the perceptions of her lover, who sees—shall we say a figment of his imagination or the real Edvarda? Behind her flagrant coquetries he discerns a fount of purity: "She has such chaste hands." Her girlish affectations, even her clumsiness, have for him a kind of appeal as of something naïve and helpless. Glahn and Edvarda are both essentially and deeply primitive though afflicted with a blight of sophistication. Each answers to a profound need in the other; each has for the other that one supreme thing which is higher and deeper than virtue and wisdom and which no one can give in its full intensity to more than one person out of the world of men and women. Both know that it is so, and yet something in

37

themselves prevents them from giving and receiving that which both long for with undying fervor. Glahn's passion is strong enough to ruin his life, but it is after all not strong enough to hold fast through good and bad, in happiness and unhappiness, and win from the relation the fullness of life which no one but Edvarda could give him. The conflict of love which Hamsun so often describes is here present in the most clearcut form because there is nothing outwardly to divide the lovers. Their tragedy is entirely of their own making.

Dagny in "Mysteries" is superficially a much more attractive young woman than Edvarda. She is the clergyman's daughter, sweet and blithe, with a big blond braid and a habit of blushing when she speaks. All the village loves her, and we can easily imagine her visiting the sick and befriending the poor. But Dagny is a far more inveterate coquette than Edvarda. While Edvarda was moved by her own thirst for excitement and longed rather to be herself subjugated than to subjugate others, Dagny is a deliberate flirt who can not bring herself to release any man once she has him in her power. Whether she loves Nagel or not he does not know, nor does the reader. She weakens for a moment under the force of his passion, but she holds fast to her purpose of marrying her handsome and wealthy fiancé, although she intrigues to prevent Martha Gude from giving Nagel what she herself withholds. That his death for her sake shakes her nature to its depths we learn when we meet her again in "Editor Lynge," where she owns to herself that at one word more she would have given up everything and thrown herself on his breast.

This one word Nagel never speaks. Like the hero of "Pan" he

seeks the haven of another woman's tenderness. He yearns toward Martha Gude with all his heart, longs for the peace and rest and purity she could have brought into his life, and yet he can not tear himself loose from the passion that binds his soul and senses. Even while he is pleading with Martha and tries to win her confidence in a scene drawn with tender delicacy, his thoughts are with Dagny, and when at last he has won Martha's shy promise, he rushes out into the night to whisper Dagny's name to the trees and the earth. The love which gushes forth irrepressibly from some unquenchable fountain in the soul, which wells out again and again, warm and fresh, however often its outlet is clogged and muddied, this love Hamsun has often pictured and seldom with more tragic force than in the unhappy hero of "Mysteries." And yet, great and real as his love is—great and real enough to send him to his death—it is not perfect. It is poisoned by a lingering doubt, which prevents him from putting forth the one last effort that would have broken down Dagny's resistance.

The lovers in Hamsun's books are never at peace. They never know the quiet, gradual opening of heart to heart or the intimate communion of perfect sympathy. With them the conflict always goes on. Gunnar Heiberg, the Norwegian dramatist, has said that there is no such thing as mutual love, because no two people ever love each other simultaneously. When one has grown warm, the other has grown cold; and when one advances, the other instinctively recoils. With Hamsun the conflict is more fine-spun than that which Heiberg has painted rather crassly. The mutual love is there, but it is a thing so wild and shy and sensitive that it shrinks back into the dark at a touch even from the hand of the beloved. Or is perhaps the human soul so jealous of its freedom that it reacts against having another individuality fasten upon it even in love?

It is these intangible forces rather than the outer facts that divide the lovers in "Victoria." Victoria is the patrician among Hamsun's heroines, not only because of her birth and breeding, but by virtue of her character. She is far too noble for deliberate coquetry, and yet she tortures Johannes by an apparent capriciousness that seems out of keeping with her frank, generous nature, while he answers with coldness and hauteur. Why? Victoria has the secret, agonizing consciousness of the promise she has given her father that she would marry a wealthy suitor who can retrieve the fallen fortunes of the family. Johannes feels his own humble birth and his distance from the princess of his dreams. Yet these reasons seem hardly sufficient. It is difficult to imagine that battered old aristocrat, Victoria's father, forcing his daughter into an unhappy marriage to save his home, still more difficult to picture the mother, who knows everything, leading her daughter to the sacrifice. Moreover, Johannes, though of humble birth, has won fame and has developed into a man of substantive personality. He is not only Victoria's lover but her playmate and oldest friend and a favorite of her parents. In fact the sweetness in the relation between cottage and manor is one of the things that entitle "Victoria" to its reputation as the most idyllic among its author's works. Why then do not these four people face the situation together? Why does not at least Victoria talk it over with her lover? Afterwards she writes that she has been hindered by many things but most by her own nature which leads her to be cruel to herself. But the real reason is that Hamsun's art at this stage of his development has no use for fulfillment. With fulfillment comes indifference. It is his to paint the unslaked thirst and the unstilled longing. Therefore the wonderful letter in which Victoria lays bare her heart is not sent until after her death, and therefore she leaves Johannes the legacy of a great tragic feeling which is forever alive and throbbing because it is forever unsatisfied.

Mariane Holmengraa in "Segelfoss City" belongs with Hamsun's young heroines. She has some traits both of Edvarda and of Victoria. But in this much later book the author has begun to take a godfatherly attitude toward his young hero and heroine; their sparring is playful rather than tragic, and he leaves them at the entrance to what promises to be a happy-ever-afterwards.

In "Munken Vendt" the man's waywardness and the woman's pride divide the two who should have belonged to each other. When Iselin, the great lady of Os, stoops to befriend the vagabond student, he tells her brutally that he has no use for her kindness and does not love her. Many years later, when he returns after a long absence, he again rejects her advances. In revenge Iselin orders him to be bound to a tree with uplifted arms until the seed in his hand has sprouted. Munken Vendt bears the torture without a murmur and curses those who would release him before she gives the word, but his hands are crippled by the ordeal, and, partly in consequence of his helplessness, he meets death not long after by an accident. Then Iselin walks backward over the edge of a pier and is drowned. Here the conflict, which appears more veiled in Hamsun's other books, is clearly expressed in terms of savage, impulsive actions possible only in a primitive state of society.

41

A relation of perfect trust and harmony is that of Isak and Inger in "Growth of the Soil." From their elemental community of interest develops a really beautiful affection, which Inger's straying from the straight path can not long disturb. It is almost as though the author would say: So simple and so primitive must people be in order to make a success of marriage for the complex and the sophisticated there is no such thing as happiness in love. A similar lesson might be drawn from "The Last Joy" where Ingeborg Torsen, a teacher, after various adventures, marries a peasant and becomes happy in sharing his humble work and bearing his children.

The rebellion of a man against the monotony of marriage has been presented again and again by writers great and small from every possible angle. The inner revolt of a woman against the concrete fact of marriage, even with the man she has herself chosen, has not often been pictured, and rarely with the sympathetic divination that Hamsun brings to bear on the subject. Puzzling and contradictory, but very interesting is, for instance, Fru Adelheid in "Children of the Age." She is a woman with a cold manner but with a warmth of temperament revealed only in her voice. At first we do not know whether she is attracted to her husband or repelled by him until she reveals that she has simply reacted against his air of possession. Her husband, the "lieutenant" of Segelfoss manor, knows that his wife has enthralled his soul and senses and that no other woman can mean anything to him, but he can not bring himself to try to patch up what has been broken. Here we have the conflict between two people of maturer years who wake up one day to the realization that it is too late. Life has passed them by and can never be recaptured.

In "Wanderers" the disintegrating influence in the marriage of the Falkenbergs is habit that breeds indifference, and Fru Falkenberg, one of Hamsun's most poignantly beautiful and most unhappy heroines, is of too fine a caliber to survive the bruise to her self-respect. In "Shallow Soil" Hanka Tidemand is drawn by the false glamour of genius which surrounds the poet Irgens, and regards her husband as nothing but a commonplace business man. Here, however, the strength and depth of the man's love saves the situation. In its happy ending their story is unique among the author's earlier works.

Among his many wayward heroines Hamsun has painted one woman of calm and benignant steadfastness, Rosa, the heroine of the two Nordland novels, "Benoni" and "Rosa." She is so deeply and innately faithful that she not only clings for many years to her worthless fiancé and finally marries him, but even after she has been forced to divorce him and has been told he is dead, she feels that she can "never be unmarried from" the man whose wife she has once been. It is only after he is really dead and after her child is born that she can be content in her marriage with her devoted old suitor, Benoni. Then the mother instinct, which is her strongest characteristic, awakens and enfolds not only her child but her child's father. Quite alone in the sisterhood of Hamsun heroines stands Martha Gude, a spinster of forty with white hair and young eyes and a child heart. Her goodness and her purity, which has the dewy freshness of morning, draw Nagel to her, although she is twelve years older than he.

Side by side and often intermingled with the ethereal delicacy of his love passages, Hamsun has many pages of such crassness that often, at the first reading of his books, they seem to overshadow and blot out the fineness. He treats the subject of sex sometimes with brutal Old Testament directness, sometimes with a rough, caustic humor akin to that of "Tom Jones" or "Tristam Shandy," but never with sultry eroticism or with innuendo under the guise of morality. There is in his very earthiness something that brings its own cleansing, as water is cleansed by passing through the ground. Probably most of us would willingly have spared from his pages many passages in "Benoni" and "Rosa," "The Last Joy," and more especially in his last book "Women at the Pump," and even in "Growth of the Soil," but they all belong to the author's conception of a true picture of life.

"What was love?" writes Johannes in "Victoria." "A wind soughing in the roses, no, a yellow phosphorescence. Love was music hot as hell which made even the hearts of old men dance. It was like the marguerite which opens wide at the approach of night, and it was like the anemone which closes at a breath and dies at a touch.

"Such was love.

"It could ruin a man, raise him up, and brand him again; it could love me to-day, you to-morrow, and him to-morrow night, so fickle was it. But it could also hold fast like an unbreakable seal and glow unquenchably in the hour of death, so everlasting was it. What then was love?

"Oh, love it was like a summer night with stars in the heavens and fragrance on earth.

But why does it make the youth go on secret paths, and why

does it make the old man stand on tiptoe in his lonely chamber? Alas, love makes the human heart into a garden of toadstools, a luxuriant and shameless garden in which secret and immodest toadstools grow.

"Does it not make the monk sneak by stealth through closed gardens and put his eye to the windows of sleepers at night? And does it not strike the nun with foolishness and darken the understanding of the princess? It lays the head of the king low on the road so that his hair sweeps all the dust of the road, and he whispers indecent words to himself and sticks his tongue out.

"Such was love.

"No, no, it was something very different again, and it was like no other thing in all the world. It came to earth on a night in spring when a youth saw two eyes, two eyes. He gazed and saw. He kissed a mouth, then it was as if two lights had met in his heart, as a sun that struck lightning from a star. He fell in an embrace, then he heard and saw nothing more in all the world.

"Love is God's first word, the first thought that passed through his brain. When he said: Let there be light! then love came. And all that he had made was very good, and he would have none of it unmade again. And love became the origin of the world and the ruler of the world. But all its ways are full of blossoms and blood, blossoms and blood."

GOD IN NATURE

The fervent love of nature which vibrates through everything Hamsun has written has endeared him to many of his countrymen who are repelled by his eroticism and out of sympathy with his social theories. The lyric rhapsodies in "Pan" minister to a deep and real craving in the Norwegian temperament, and it is not for nothing that this book has steadfastly held its own as the first in the affections of the public. "Fair is the valley; never saw I it fairer," said Gunnar of Hlidarendi in "Njal's Saga," when he turned from the ship he had made ready to carry him away from his Iceland home, and went back to face certain death there rather than save himself by banishment. To the Northerner, whether he be Icelander, Swede, or Norwegian, natural environment is the determining influence in the choice of his home; and not only the poet and artist but the average middle class individual, clerk, teacher, or store-keeper, will forego social life and endure much discomfort in order to establish himself in a place where he can satisfy the love of beauty in nature which is one of the strongest passions in the Northern races. And yet, however fair the valley of his home, he will yearn to get away from it sometimes, to rove alone on skis over the snowfields or bury himself in a forest hut far from the sound of a human voice. The vast uncultivated stretches of Norway have enabled the people to follow their bent and seek outdoor solitude, and while the habit has not fostered in them the pleasant urban virtues of nations that live more in cities, it has developed a richness and intensity of inner life which has flowered vividly in their art and literature.

The solitary hunter of "Pan" is perhaps the most typically Norwegian among the Hamsun heroes, and in him love of nature has deepened into a veritable passion. This book, which followed several novels of city and town life and was written during a summer in Norway after a sojourn abroad, is the first full-toned expression of Hamsun's feeling for nature. It has a melting tenderness and a warm intimacy of knowledge which can only come from much living out of doors, as the author did when he herded cattle as a boy, and later when he roved through the country as a vagrant laborer. To read it is like nothing else but lying on your back and gazing up to the mountains until you feel the breath of the forest as your own breath and sense no stirring of life except that which sways the trees above you. The feeling of being one with nature, of enfolding all things with affection and being oneself enfolded in a universal goodness, is typical of Hamsun's attitude. He never paints nature merely as the scenic background for his human drama, and he never romances about nature for its own sake. He rarely describes in detail; it is as though he were too near for description. Like a child which buries its face on its mother's breast and does not know whether her features are homely or beautiful, he seems to be hiding his face in the grass and listening to the pulse-beats of the earth rather than standing off and looking at it. "I seem to be lying face to face with the bottom of the universe," says Glahn, as he gazes into a clear sunset sky, "and my heart seems to beat tenderly against this bottom and to be at home here." Nothing is great or small to him. A boulder in the road fills him with such a sense of friendliness that he goes back every day and feels as though he were being welcomed home. A blade of grass trembling in the sun suffuses his soul with an infinite sea of tenderness.

"Pan" is full of lyric outbursts. When Glahn revisits the forest on the first spring day, he is moved to transports. He weeps with love and joy and is dissolved in thankfulness to all living things. He calls the birds and trees and rocks by name; nay, even the beetles and worms are his friends. The mountains seem to call to him, and he lifts his head to answer them. He can sit for hours listening to the tiny drip, drip of the water that trickles down the face of the rocks, singing its own melody year in and year out, and this faint stirring of life fills his soul with contentment.

Glahn follows the intense seasonal changes of Nordland. At midsummer, when the sun hardly dips its golden ball in the sea at night, he sees all nature intoxicated with sex, rushing on to fruition in the few short weeks of summer. Then mysterious fancies come over him. He weaves a strange tale about Iselin, the mistress of life, the spirit of love, who lives in the forest. He dreams that she comes to him and tells about her first love. The breath of the forest is like her breath, and he feels her kisses on his lips, and the stars sing in his blood. The women who meet him in the forest, Eva and the little goat-girl, seem to him only a part of nature as they expand unconsciously to love like the flower in the sun, and he takes what they give him. Yet there is in him a spiritual craving which these loves of the forest can not satisfy.

Summer passes; the first nipping sense of autumn is in the air, and the children of nature too feel the benumbing hand of coming winter, as if the brief thrill of summer in their veins had already subsided. But in the solitude of the dark, cold "iron nights" the Northern Pan wins from Nature the highest she has to give him. As he sits alone, he gives thanks for "the lonely night, for the mountains, the darkness, and the throbbing ocean.... This stillness that murmurs in my ear is the blood of all nature that is seething. God who vibrates through the world and me."

Though "Pan" is Hamsun's first great rapturous hymn to nature, his earlier novel "Mysteries" contains some beautiful passages that may be considered a prelude to it. Nagel is absorbed in the affairs of men and smitten with the modern social unrest. He lives the life of books and thoughts and is no half-savage hunter like Glahn, but he seeks in nature the sense of vastness and infinity that his soul longs for. He loves to lie on his back and feel himself sailing off into the sea of heaven. "He lost himself in a transport of contentment. Nothing disturbed him, but up in the air the soft sound went on, the sound of an immense stamping-mill, God who trod his wheel. But in the woods round about him there was not a stir, not a leaf or a pine-needle moved. Nagel curled up with pleasure, drew his knees up under him, and shivered with a sense of how good it all was.... He was in a strange frame of mind, filled with psychic pleasure. Every nerve in him was alive, he felt music in his blood, felt himself akin to nature and the sun and the mountains and everything else, felt himself caught up in a vibration of his own ego from trees and hillocks and blades of grass. His soul expanded and was like a full-toned organ within him. He never forgot how the soft music literally rose and fell with the pulsing of his blood."

As in "Pan" and "Mysteries," so in his other books Hamsun makes us feel the moods of nature through those of his people. In "Victoria" we are always conscious of the colorful background of heather and rowan and sparkling blue sea because the minds of Johannes and Victoria are steeped in the beauty of the land where they have played as children. In the big Nordland novels, on the other hand, we meet people who take no direct interest in their natural environments, and here the author is more chary of his nature lyricism. The careless, childish, volatile fisherfolk and day labourers in "Benoni" and "Rosa" and in "Segelfoss Town" take the glory of the sea and the cliffs with their swarms of white-winged birds very much for granted and have nothing to say about them, but unconsciously their life rises and falls with the seasons. "It was spring again" is the almost invariable prelude to action in the Nordland novels. The warm nights had come; the red sunlight was over sea and land; the boys and girls went about singing and laughing and flirting the whole night long, and even the old felt the stirring of youth in their blood, the unquenchable old villain Mack got "the strong look" in his eyes again, and poor old Holmengraa went on devious paths. There is a glamour and a fairy-tale atmosphere always resting over Nordland summers, but when autumn comes, a numbed torpor steals over everything, as if people, like nature, were only lying dormant waiting for spring to wake them again.

Even that glamour which redeems the littleness in "Segelfoss City" has died in "Women at the Pump," the author's latest book, in which he depicts the petty mean, degenerate people of a small town that seems afflicted with dry rot, and the total absence of feeling for nature has much to do with the grey and rayless effect of this novel. In "Growth of the Soil," on the other hand, there is a wonderful sense of the nearness of nature. Isak could not put his reflections into words, but a simple awe takes possession of him in the loneliness of the forest and the moors, where he "meets God." As Geissler expresses it, the plain people of Sellanraa meet nature bare-handed in the midst of a great friendliness, and the mountains stand around and look at them.

Yet Hamsun's feeling for nature is by no means a mere primitive emotion; it is rather the reasoned expression of a man who has found his way back to the real sources of life. In its subtlest and most artistic form it appears in the "Wanderer" books. The overemphasis and extravagance which could, in "Pan," verge on the hysterical are gone, and instead there is a mellow sweetness, a poignant tenderness as of a man who knows that his own autumn has arrived and that winter is on the way. It is Indian summer in the opening chapter of "Under the Autumn Star." The air is mild and warm and tranquil, everything breathes peace after the brief, intense effort of summer to put forth growth. Round about stand the red rowans and the stiff-necked flowers refusing to know that fall is here. In these paragraphs the keynote of the book is given, and throughout this book and its sequel, "A Wanderer Plays with Muted. Strings," the harmony with nature is preserved. For all the charm of the story and the pungency of the reflections on various themes, that which lingers in the reader's mind is the long autumn road, the nights in the fragrant hayloft, the smell of freshly felled trees, and the fire in the woods where the Wanderer is alone at last with nature.

Hamsun loves the warm, expansive moods of nature and has confessed to a positive dislike of ice and snow. Descriptions of winter are rare in his books, but the opening chapter of "The Last Joy" finds the Wanderer snowbound in a hut far up in the mountains, and although he watches the spring awakening of nature, he knows that in his own life winter has come to stay. For that very reason he feels as never before a great upwelling of affection for all things around him, animate and inanimate. He can sit for hours merely watching the course of the sun, or speculating about some tiny bug which was born and will probably die on the one leaf it inhabits, or marvelling at the wonder of reproduction in a little plant that is releasing its seed. A lonely little path straggling through the forest affects him like a child's hand in his own. A lacerated pine stump rouses his pity as he stands gazing at it until his other, civilized self reminds him that his eyes have probably acquired the simple animal expression of people in the Stone Age. He walks over a hillside and feels a tenderness emanating from it. "It is not really a hillside, it is a bosom, a lap, so soft is it, and I walk carefully and do not tramp heavily on it with my feet. I am filled with wonder at it: a great hillside so tender and helpless that it allows us to use it as a mother, allows an ant to crawl over it. If there is a boulder half covered with grass, it has not just happened here; it lives here and has lived here long."

As he walks on, he begins to feel a strange influence about him. "Something vibrates softly in me, and it seems to me as so often before out of doors that the place has just been left, that some one has just been here and has stepped aside. At this moment I am alone with some one here, and a little later I see a back that vanishes in the forest. It is God, I say to myself. There I stand, I do not speak, I do not sing, I only look. I feel that my face is filled with the vision. It was God, I say to myself. A figment of the imagination, you will reply. No, a little insight into things, I say. Do I make a god of nature? What do you do? Have not the Mohammedans their god and the Jews their god and the Hindoos their god? No one knows God, my little friend, men only know gods. Now and then it seems to me that I meet mine."

In one of his oriental travel sketches Hamsun has said that unlike most people he never gets through with God, but feels the need of brooding over him under the starry heavens and listening for his voice in the breath of the forest. In "The Last Joy" the sense of God in nature is always present in the background of the narrator's thoughts. In the great stillness, where he is the only human being, he feels himself expanding into something greater than himself, he becomes God's neighbor. The last joy is to retire and sit alone in the woods and feel the friendly darkness closing around him. "It is the lofty and religious element in solitude and darkness that makes us crave them. It is not that we want to get away from other people because we can not bear to have any one near us—no, no! But it is the mysterious sense that everything is rushing in on us from afar, and yet all is near, so that we sit in the midst of an omnipresence. Perhaps it is God."

WITH MUTED STRINGS

The superiority of youth over age has been a cardinal doctrine with Hamsun. How seriously he has taken it is best shown by the fact that four of his plays and three of his novels are devoted to the theme. First in point of time is the dramatic trilogy, "At the Gate of the Kingdom" (1895), "The Game of Life" (1896), and "Sunset" (1898), presenting three stages in the life of the philosopher Kareno. Of later date are the three novels, "Under the Autumn Star" (1906), "A Wanderer Plays with Muted Strings" (1909), and "The Last Joy" (1912), each marking a milestone in the progress of the Wanderer toward the land of old age. Quite alone stands "In the Power of Life" (1910), a drama which shows an aging courtezan desperately trying to retain a few shreds of her power over men.

Kareno, a native of Nordland, has Lapp blood in his veins, which may in part account for the latent weakness that comes out in him as soon as the strong impetus of youth has died down. At twenty-nine he rushes into print gallantly to attack the prevailing ideals of his day, such as eternal peace, the apotheosis of labor, the humanitarian efforts to preserve life however worthless, and in general the gods of liberalism. Spencer and Stuart Mill, who were at that time names to conjure with, he called mediocrities devoid of inspiration. His most violent onslaughts were reserved for the doctrine that youth should honor old age. For these theories he sacrificed wife and home, career and friends.

In the following play we find him, now thirty-nine, as tutor to a rich man's children in Nordland. His intellect is already befuddled. By means of a glass house provided with powerful lenses, which his patron is helping him to build and equip, he is trying to achieve by material, technical contrivances the clarity which, after all, he has proved himself unable to evolve from within. His moral fibre too is weakened. At twenty-nine he allowed his young wife to leave him rather than temporize with his conscience; now he becomes absorbed in a passion for his patron's daughter, Teresita, a wanton, capricious woman of the Edvarda type but without Edvarda's sweetness. Formerly he refused to save his home from impending catastrophe by a proferred loan from his comrade Jerven, because the money was the fruit of Jerven's apostacy from their common cause; now he is ready to accept bounty from any source.

A fire which consumes his house and manuscripts terminates his work in Nordland, and we hear no more of him, before, in the last of the three plays, we find him in Christiania again. He is now fifty, and his deterioration is complete. He is settling down to a life of smug Philistine contentment, enjoying the fortune which his wife has in the meantime inherited, and accepting the daughter who is the fruit of his wife's unfaithfulness rather than quarrel with the comforts she provides for him. Kareno has

55

somehow managed to preserve a semblance of his former fire and with it a reputation for prowess as a dauntless fighter, but in his heart he is already out of sympathy with the cause of youth and ready to turn traitor at the first beckoning of really substantial honors.

The other characters have gone through the same process of dissolution. Jerven has continued his inevitable downward course. His one time fiancée, Miss Hovind, who broke with him because of his apostacy, has become a silly old maid who glories in her former connection with the famous professor. Only Höibro, the man outside the parties who is still at variance with everything accepted, has kept himself at fifty-one unspotted from the world.

The weakness of the trilogy lies partly in the character of Kareno which shows not so much the softening of fibre due to old age as the revelation of a latent meanness, and partly in the nature of the principles for which he is expected to sacrifice himself. It is true that he feels in his youth the reality of the spiritual above the temporal, and in the face of impending ruin he can say: "It is as though I had been alone on earth last night. There is a wall between human beings and that which is outside them, but this wall is now worn thin, and I will try to break it down, to knock my head through it and see. And see!" But what he sees is only temporalities, not eternal verities. Granted that the liberal movement had become stale and needed a renewal, there was nothing in that fact to create a supreme issue. It was one of many movements that have run and will run their natural course till the inevitable reaction sets in. There was no great scientific truth or fiery religious passion involved, nothing to call forth a Galileo

56

or a Luther. As with Kareno, so with Jerven and Miss Hovind. A girl who breaks with her lover because he weakens in his denunciations of Spencer and Stuart Mill is a strain on the reader's credulity.

There is only one of the vaunted principles in the trilogy which has a universal application, namely the doctrine that a man at fifty is useless and should resign his place to the young, but this doctrine Kareno can hardly be expected to hold with the same uncompromising rigor at fifty as at twenty-nine.

The whole situation therefore becomes farcical, and we can hardly wonder that the middle-aged philosopher wipes his brow when his young quondam admirer reads in his ear the following quotation from his own early works:

"What do you demand of the young? That they shall honor the old. Why? The doctrine was invented by decrepit age itself. When age could no longer assert itself in the struggle for life, it did not go away and hide its diminished head, but made itself broad in exalted places and commanded the young to do honor and pay homage to it. And when the young obeyed, the old sat up like big sexless birds gloating over the docility of youth. Listen, you who are young! Set a match under the old and clear the seat and take your place, for yours is the power and the glory for ever and ever.... When the old speak, the young are expected to be silent. Why? Because the old have said it. So age continues to lead its protected, carefree existence at the expense of youth. The old hearts are dead to everything except hatred for the new and the young. And in the worn-out brains there is still strength left for one more idea, a sly idea: that youth shall honor toothlessness. And while the young are hampered and thwarted in their development by this cynical doctrine, the victors themselves sit and gloat over their marvellous invention and think life is very fine indeed."

Written while Hamsun was yet under forty, the three Kareno plays are an aftermath of his own struggles as a young man to break into the ring of the accepted. They are an outcry against the older men who had once been iconoclasts, but had standardized their iconoclasm, who had once been advocates of free thought, but had forged free thought into a weapon to strike down all who differed from themselves. It is therefore no accident that Kareno's onslaughts are directed against a stereotyped liberalism. The trilogy is significant as a subjective expression of a certain phase in the author's development, but in psychological interest it is far inferior to the Wanderer books. In these Hamsun has rid himself of all bitterness and has found a sweet and mellow tone that is singularly appealing. He is no longer a theorist but a poet, that is he is himself at his best and highest. He no longer vaunts a principle but portrays a human being.

The Wanderer is a man who renounces the cafés and boulevards and, after eighteen years of city life, revisits the haunts of his youth disguised as a vagrant laborer. Thus he divests himself of whatever pomp and circumstance surround a successful middle-aged man and well known citizen, in order to meet youth on equal terms simply as Knud Pedersen, a man whose muscles are a little stiff and whose beard is getting grey. "Under the Autumn Star" and "A Wanderer Plays with Muted Strings," bound together in the English edition under the common title

"Wanderers," relate experiences lying five or six years apart. In the first the narrator is nearing fifty; in the second he has passed the mark. The Wanderer in "Under the Autumn Star" is still full of vim and vigor, loves to feel his contact with the soil again, and glories in his prowess, notably in the invention of a wonderful saw which absorbs him. He becomes enamored of Fru Falkenberg, wife of the captain on whose estate he has taken service, and is young enough to make frantic attempts to win her, even throwing off his disguise and appearing in his own character; but when she begs him not to pursue her, he desists.

Some years later his longing drives him again to the Falkenberg estate, but now he is in a different frame of mind. He "plays with muted strings." He still works with his old energy, but his invention, the marvellous saw, has become "literature" to him. Women are "literature." He makes no attempt to approach Fru Falkenberg, but from his obscure place among her other servants he watches mournfully her gradual deterioration and philosophizes over the causes that led to it. The captain and his wife have drifted apart from sheer idleness, because they have no separate pursuits that might take them away from each other and give their hours together the freshness of reunions. In the earlier book, the wife, though she is drifting hither and thither on the breath of longing and discontent, is so essentially true that she feels even the homage of her humble admirer as a danger which she must flee from. When the Wanderer comes back, the idle years have done their work on her. "She had nothing to do, but she had three maids in her house; she had no children, but she had a piano. But she had no children," muses the Wanderer. But while he himself keeps the distance she has

59

imposed upon him, he sees a younger, more brazen admirer pushing himself into her favor. The scruples that bind the man past fifty have no existence for the youth of twenty-two. The Wanderer feels no passion of jealousy, but only a great weary lassitude and loneliness. He knows that for him it is evening. He grieves over her ruin, but can do nothing to avert it. All he can do is to put his whole heart into the humble task of preparing her home against her possible return, helping the captain to paint and refurnish the house. His efforts are of no avail; Fru Falkenberg returns to her husband, but too many fine threads have been broken, and their life together proves impossible.

After her death the Wanderer seeks the solitude of a forest hut, and there he sits looking over his life in retrospect after the fashion of those who know that life is chiefly behind them. "I remember a lady, she guarded nothing, least of all herself. She came to such a bad end. But six or seven years ago I had never believed that any one could be so fine and lovely to another person as she was. I drove her carriage on a journey, and she was bashful before me, although she was my mistress; she blushed and looked down. And the strange thing was that she made me too bashful before her, although I was her servant. Only by looking at me with her two eyes when she gave me an order she revealed to me beauties and values beyond all those I had known before. I remember it even now. Yes. I am sitting here and thinking of it yet, and I shake my head and say to myself: How strange it was, no, no, no! And then she died. What more? Then there is no more. I am left. But that she died ought not to grieve me; I had been paid in advance for that when, without my deserving it, she looked at me with her two eyes." A middle-aged sigh breathes through these words, the sigh of a man who has known life and felt it to be good and who is not avid for more. He is a letter that has arrived and is no longer on the way; that which matters is whether its contents have brought joy or sorrow or whether they have fallen to the ground without making any impression. He has come too late to the berryfields, and there is no more to be said. His only hope is that he may never become senile enough to imagine himself wise because he is old.

The two volumes contained in "Wanderers" are among the most finished of Hamsun's production. I have already spoken of the harmony between nature and the moods of men. In the human drama, too, the artistic unity is always preserved. It is held throughout in low tones, and while the Wanderer enters so well into his rôle that we sometimes forget he is not really a common laborer, we are never allowed to forget his age. We are always conscious of the gentle enervation stealing over his faculties and the gradual loosening of his hold on life. He becomes all the time less and less of a participant in the story, more and more of an onlooker.

In "The Last Joy" old age is no longer standing at the door; it has come in and laid its hand upon him. "I am driven by fire and fettered by ice," writes the Wanderer in the hut where he has retired to make the big irons within him glow. In truth he is not sure whether he still has any irons or whether he can still heat them. The ideas that once rushed in upon him with overwhelming force now come only at the cost of painstaking labor. Bodily work too has become irksome to him, and when he begins to long for intercourse with other people, he does not, like the Wanderer in the earlier books, hire himself out to service, but goes to spend some idle months at a tourist hotel. There he learns that his heart is not too old to give him trouble, when he falls in love with Ingeborg Torsen. He is attracted by her brilliant beauty and glowing vitality, and he looks at her waywardness with a deep and tender comprehension which no young man could have given her. No doubt he might have won her, but he is restrained by the horror of being grotesque and indulging in antics unbefitting his age. So he stands by, and again he is fated to see the woman he loves ruining herself. But Ingeborg Torsen is of tougher fibre than Fru Falkenberg, and she saves herself in a marriage which brings her children and heavy household cares. The Wanderer has played the rôle of her fatherly friend and confidant, but at last he realizes that she does not need him any more even in this capacity. The knowledge hurts, but not for very long, and not very severely. His feeling for her has been real, the loss of her leaves him a little more sad and lonely than before, but love with him is no longer the inexorable, devastating passion that sent Glahn and Nagel to their death.

Hamsun has essayed in "Wanderers" and "The Last Joy" to show the enervating influence of the years. Again and again he tells us that age can add nothing but only take away, that age is not ripeness, it is just age—just toothlessness. Yet the impression left on the reader's mind is that of a personality gradually being detached, first from the fetters of its own passions, then from absorption in other people, and finding at last freedom in loneliness.

THE LITERARY ARTIST

The time immediately preceding Hamsun's authorship was, in Norway, a period of revolt. All the established canons of public and private morality were being questioned, and literature was made a platform of debate in a manner never before known. No poet who respected himself was content to be merely a songster. He felt it incumbent upon him to be a thinker and a prophet, a moralist and a reformer. Hence every new novel or drama that appeared propounded some opinion on free love or marriage, the doctrines of the established church, the upheaval of the social order, the position of women, the reform of the school system, or other topic of timely discussion. To realize the change that had come over literature we need only compare Ibsen in "Brand" with Ibsen in "Ghosts." In the former he probed the human heart, laid bare the weaknesses that are common to humanity under all conditions, and gave poetic form to the ideals that are the same in all ages. In the latter he took up a special pathological problem on which his knowledge could be called in question by any medical expert. In the same vein, Kielland, the creator of the inimitable Skipper Worse, devoted his talents to demonstrating in a novel the evils of silence regarding venereal diseases. Björnson was perhaps the worst offender of all, and yet his preaching was salved by such a broad and warm humanity that his pedantry could be forgiven. Among his novels of the period, "The Kurt Family," which begins with tremendous power, dribbles out into a treatise on hygiene and morality, but happily the artist in Björnson is too big to be confined within the limits he has set himself, and occasionally he bursts out into delightful scenes. In the end, however, we leave Thomas Rendalen and Nora clasping hands over a mission instead of making love in the old-fashioned way. In "A Gauntlet" Björnson lets Svava formulate the single standard of morality; in "A Bankruptcy" he takes up the subject of business integrity, and so on. Among the great creative writers, Jonas Lie and Garborg escaped comparatively unscathed, Jonas Lie because he never could abandon his habit of portraying life instead of reasoning about it, and Garborg because he saved himself in time by going back to the soil and the peasantry, where he discovered a fountain of poetic renewal. The lesser authors followed the lead of Björnson and Ibsen in their less happy vein and without their genius. The whole tendency, which, to begin with, had had the freshness of revolt, of indignation, and of hope, was becoming smug and standardized.

A scapegoat had to be found for the ills from which the authors' heroes and heroines were suffering, and Ibsen named it in "A Doll's House," when he let Nora lay the blame for her foolishness on "society"—reasoning so out of keeping with the character of the childish, irresponsible Nora that we can not help wondering how Ibsen ever made it sound plausible. It was accepted because it fell in with the prevailing mood of the day. If only society could be reorganized after a pattern on the reformers' nail all would be well! They forgot what seems to us at this day obvious to the point of banality, namely that when Nora had taken a full course in commercial arithmetic, and Svava had vowed to die unwed, and all the little Millas and Toras and Thinkas in good Fru Rendalen's school had learned all about the pitfalls that awaited them, there would still be the devastating power of love; and when everybody had a job so that young men could marry at the natural time and young women need not marry except for love, there would still be those sudden, erratic attractions and repulsions which work havoc and create tragedies under the most well-ordered conditions. Moreover, they forgot that, although the wrongs which cry out for reform may be susceptible to artistic treatment, the reforms themselves, circumscribing as they do ideals by finite achievement, are not food meet for the imaginative writer. A reformed Marshalsea would not have given us any Little Dorrit. In Norwegian literature, Jonas Lie painted a gallery of splendid women whose grandeur of outline is thrown into relief by the pettiness of their surroundings; his Inger-Johanne and Cecilie are tragic figures when they beat their wings against the bars of convention, but when a later generation of writers attempted to send Inger-Johanne to normal school and let Cecilie learn typewriting, the romance was dead.

Against this whole school of literature with its absorption in types and causes Hamsun protested with all his youthful vehemence and all his power of drastic ridicule. It would not be correct to say that he advocated a return to the principle of art for art's sake. Indeed he has used his own literary work as the vehicle of any opinion that pressed for utterance in him, from his reflections on the state of Norwegian literature in "Mysteries" to those on the evils of the tourist traffic in "The Last Joy." The truth is rather that his poetic sensibilities recoiled from the smug sapience, the heavy sententiousness that would rob life of its spontaneity and reduce it to a pharmaceutical formula: so much democracy, so much popular education, so much reform legislation, and a perfect state of society would follow inevitably. He disliked the thinness and bloodlessness of a literary art that substituted reasoning for inspiration. Poets, he said, should not be philosophers; they usually philosophized very badly, as witnessed Ibsen and Tolstoy when they departed from their function as poets and began to prescribe remedies for the ills of the world. As for Björnson, he revered him not because of his activities as a preacher and a moralist, but in spite of them, because of his humanness, his irrepressibility, his endless power of growth and renewal. One of Hamsun's most beautiful poems is a homage to Björnson.

In his later years, Hamsun has himself essayed the rôle of the preacher, or, as a Norwegian critic put it, he has assumed Björnson's habit of occasionally chastising the Norwegian nation for its own good in a fatherly fashion. There is a difference, however, between him and his predecessors. They were sometimes institutional; he is always personal. They sometimes attempt to construct the world from a diagram of planes and angles; he always follows the flowing lines of the artist. Even when he preaches, his message is in its essence a part of his poetic impulse. His apotheosis of the man with the hoe springs

66

from his longing to get close to the soil and draw strength from primal sources. His impatience with all the modern army of semi-intellectual workers, the clerks and administrators who wind red tape and spoil white paper, is in keeping with his craving to brush aside all that cumbersome machinery which men interpose between the human will and the physical realities. His strident condemnation of the movements that are counted liberal in our day is a protest against the levelling which robs life of its color and sharp contrasts. His imagination demands the peaks and high lights and can find no satisfaction in the modern cult of mediocrity or the dull grey level of utilitarianism.

To Hamsun the abstraction called society, which looms so large in the liberal thought of to-day, has no existence. He sees only individuals, and this is one of the reasons why, even when he waxes didactic, he does not cease to be artistic. Isak, who is his ideal type of citizen, is also one of his great poetic creations. In his earlier and more personal work, however, the element of moralizing is absent. The typical Hamsun hero, a Glahn or a Nagel, is not to be measured with the yardstick of ordinary standards. What interests their creator is not the patent virtues and vices which can easily be catalogued, but the fugitive life-spark that defies analysis and yet is what constitutes personality. To the poet the intangible and elusive is the real, the evanescent is the stable. Why do people do thus and so? "Ask the wind and the stars. Ask the dust on the road and the leaves that fall, ask the mysterious God of life, for no one else knows."

The message of Hamsun's later works, which has swept them like a life-giving stream over a world made arid by pseudo-civilization, is: Back to nature! Back to the land! The message of

67

his earlier works was: Back to poetry! Away from problems and causes back to the dream and the vision! There is no contradiction between the two; both are equally genuine expressions of a personality which has the richness, the many-sidedness and spontaneity of life itself.

His method of artistic presentment is as fresh and unhackneyed as his subject matter. It has always been regarded as the function of the artist to separate the great from the small, the essential from the unessential, and to make a character, a human life, or an event stand out in sculptured clearness freed from the accidental and the extraneous. With this ideal in view, writers have concentrated their efforts on the great revealing scenes in the career of their heroes. Hamsun breaks entirely with this tradition. To him nothing is small or extraneous. His books are like broad surfaces rippled by many points of light, and it is only gradually that these points of light, the tiny but pregnant incidents and the flashing bits of description, separate and converge to form images. It is a part of his method in creating an illusion of life to draw his characters into the circle of our acquaintanceship, not by great dramatic scenes leading up to a climax, or by sudden opening of abysses as in Ibsen, still less by long description, but by just such scattered and casual bits of information as usually build up our knowledge of people and events in real life. Some trifle is blown in on our consciousness and finds a lodgement there; it may be a quotation or a word of comment that stirs our expectancy and prepares us to meet an individual. We see his shadow falling over the path of another person or feel his presence like a breath of wind. Perhaps we hear no more of him at the time, but in another book we meet him again, and now he is the hero, whom we follow until we think we know him like a dog-eared schoolbook—until some sudden turn upsets our theories, and we leave him in the last chapter with a baffled sense of imperfect understanding. But the author is not yet done with him. In some later book, which is not a sequel in the ordinary sense but brushes the fringes of the first, we come upon a passage that throws a backward light over the ground we have traversed. When we close "Pan," for instance, we know no more of Edvarda than her lover knows, but when we read "Rosa" we find the clue to her nature. In the same manner, Dagny, the heroine of "Mysteries," does not reveal her heart before we meet her again as one of the subordinate characters in "Editor Lynge." It is as though a figure that had once sprung from the author's brain became imbued with such vitality that it continued to live through his later works. J. P. Jacobsen once said that he was forced to let all his people die, because death was the only real end; nothing in life ever ended. Hamsun sometimes resorts to this method, but even then the dead live on in the memory of those who have known them. With him nothing is ever finished or finite.

Hamsun's humor is all-pervasive it is the yeast that lightens his loaf. When Albert Engström, the Swedish humorist, ended an appreciation of Hamsun by saying, "And finally I love you for the gleam in your left eye," he found an apt expression for the personality that shines through Hamsun's works.

His humor has less of wit than of comicality, less of the laugh than the smile with a gleam in his eye; and he is as ready to smile at his own intensities as at the weaknesses of humanity. His flights of fancy are tempered with irony, his real reverence with a playfulness that often takes the guise of impish irreverence. He loves the far-flung paradox and the sudden transition of thought by which he astonishes his readers.

The quality of unexpectedness in his thought is well simulated in the style he has evolved for himself. This style was fully developed when Hamsun made his first appearance as an author, a fact which adds interest to Sigurd Hoel's opinion that the dash and brilliance of "Hunger" was due to American influence. Certainly Hamsun has never improved upon this style, and it may even be questioned whether its manner with the light staccato touch, the prevalence of interjections and sentences consisting sometimes of a single word, has not in some of his later works hardened into a mannerism that results in a slight weariness of repetition. Taken as a whole, however, his style has been a bath of rejuvenation to Northern literature. It has the naturalness of the spoken word, following blithely the quips and pranks of thought that give zest to conversation but are usually flattened out before they reach print. The result is a light whimsicality, a capriciousness which Hamsun cultivates with subtle and conscious art, until he attains a sparkle and vividness, an ease and flexibility never before known in the language of his country.

As the literary artist Hamsun gives us apples of gold in pitchers of silver, and the metal for both is entirely of his own forging.

THE CITIZEN

HOLDING UP THE MIRROR TO HIS
GENERATION

Very early in his career as an author Hamsun struck the keynote of the message which in his most recent works he has preached with so much power. The two novels "Editor Lynge" (1893) and "Shallow Soil" (1893), satirizing certain journalistic and literary phenomena in Christiania, showed the reverse side of the ideal in which he believes, and by contrast pointed the way to new standards and new goals.

The main character in "Editor Lynge" is an intellectual parvenue, a peasant lad who has risen to the position of editor-in-chief, not by great and commanding qualities, but by a cheap smartness, a facility for shoving himself in, and a brazen self-possession that never deserts him. He is without real convictions and real courage, and yet manages to hoodwink the public into thinking him a great moral leader. A scandal-monger under pretence of defending virtue, he impudently assumes the right to pry into other people's affairs and spread them large over the pages of his paper.

71

Some of the obnoxious sides of Lynge's activity we can, of course, recognize as belonging to the dark side of daily newspaper work everywhere, although they appear with more transparent naïveté in a small country. In making him a peasant lad who had risen into another class without assimilating its standards, who attempted to be a leader without having inherited the traditions of leadership, Hamsun had in mind certain phases of a transition period in his own country. Popular education had opened the professions and government offices to country lads, but could not in a single generation give them real culture. They remained mentally homeless and rootless. In Lynge he portrays a man who has suffered an injury to his soul by a transplantation which could never be complete. Significantly enough, Lynge's most ardent admirer is another transplanted country boy, Endre Bondesen, whose origin is stamped on him in his name (Bondesen, peasant's son). He too has lost his contact with the soil and thereby lost the standards of conduct in his own class without acquiring those in the class he has entered. Their attitude toward the new possibilities that open before them Hamsun describes as a kind of triumphant snicker: "Tee-hee-hee! what great fellows we are!"

The author of "Hunger," who a few years earlier had described the purgatory prepared for the young genius who is struggling to get into print and to live on the proceeds of his work, did not have to go far afield for the caustic sting with which he scourged the people who make themselves broad in the inner courts of journalism and literature. In "Editor Lynge" he parodied the vaunted power of the press. In "Shallow Soil" he painted a picture of the small geniuses who pose on street corners and in cafés and bask in the popular admiration that is liberally

72

bestowed on even the thinnest rinsings from the wine-glass of genius. The little poets and artists regard themselves as divinely exempted from all the sordid but necessary work of the world, and believe their own slight productions are sufficient excuse for a parasitical life in vice and idleness. There is Öien who is so exhausted after squeezing out of his brain a few small prose poems that he has to be sent to a sanitarium at the expense of his friends, and there is Irgens, the only one who seems actually to bring forth a real book occasionally, using his privilege as a poet to live on the bounty of friends whom he is playing false in the most dastardly way. With them is a crowd of idlers and revellers whose chief ambition is to find some one who will pay for their next meal.

As a contrast to this despicable coterie Hamsun has not raised up a real genius like his own alter ego in "Hunger," but two young business men whom he uses to point the moral of regular work and contact with actualities as the great salvation of modern civilization. The keynote is struck in the opening chapter with a finely-etched picture of the awakening city, when Irgens with waxed mustache and patent leather shoes is strolling home from a night of debauch and finds Ole Henriksen, alert and clear-eyed, already at his desk in his father's big office on the dock, and fortunately able to spare the ten krone bill which the poet needs.

Ole Henriksen and his friend Andreas Tidemand, in their moral cleanliness, their modesty and chivalry, their loyalty to each other and generosity to their friends, are not unlike the ideal young business hero of American novels, but they are afflicted with the cult of genius which was prevalent in their country at the time. They like to be seen dining at the Grand with poets and painters and actors, and gladly assume the privilege of paying the bills for the crowd, while, with a simplicity that borders on gullibility, they allow the one his wife and the other his fiancée to be decoyed away from them by the enterprising poet Irgens. Hanka Tidemand, a really sweet and chaste nature, has accustomed herself to the rôle of sympathizing with genius, and when she gives herself to Irgens it is almost with a sense of being a pious burnt-offering on the altar of his poetry. Aagot, a fresh, pretty country girl, one of Hamsun's brightest and youngest heroines, is dazzled by the glamour of the literary circle into which she is introduced, and becomes the poet's next victim. Hanka awakens to a realization that it is her husband whom she loves and returns to him. Aagot, with less stamina, is completely demoralized, and Ole Henriksen shoots himself rather than survive the old Aagot, the innocent Aagot, whom he had loved.

"Shallow Soil" is perhaps to a greater extent than any of Hamsun's other works based on certain local conditions and phases of development in his own country. The cult of pseudo-genius which it ridicules is not so prevalent among us that its satire can come home to us as it did to the author's countrymen. The book will always appeal, however, by virtue of its literary qualities. The critic Carl Morburger calls it Hamsun's most finished literary masterpiece. The subtle delineation of character, the vividness in the portrayal of contrasting personalities, and the fresh, natural tone save it from the sententiousness into which a novel with so evident a purpose would have fallen in the hands of a lesser artist.

The two friends Ole Henriksen and Andreas Tidemand, who are

chosen to illustrate the mental and moral tone acquired from practical work, are both merchants. It is the occupation which, next to husbandry, makes the greatest appeal to the author's imagination. He does not, however, tell us much of the achievements of his heroes. His idea of the merchant's business as the life-giving artery of a district is not developed until many years later in the wonderfully ramified pictures of whole communities, usually with a Nordland background, in which the trading magnate nearly always occupies the centre of the stage.

In "Pan" we first encounter the great Mack family which pervades the Nordland novels. Edvarda's father, the master of Sirilund, is something of a fop with his diamond shirt studs and his pointed shoes among the boulders, and rather more of a villain, a man to whom the neighborhood pays its tribute of wives and maidens as a Zulu tribe to its chieftain, but for all that a small superman by whose brains the community exists. In "Dreamers" (1904) we see at close range his still greater brother Mack of Rosengaard, who hovers like a fairy-tale in the background of the other books. But Mack of Sirilund is one of the characters that Hamsun has not been able to leave, and, fourteen years after the publication of "Pan," we meet him again in "Benoni" (1908) and "Rosa" (1908). He is a providence and a small god to the simple people of the neighborhood. Whatever else falls, Mack stands impregnable as a rock. His existence among them is an earnest that somehow the world will go on, even if the fishing fails, and boats are lost at sea. Whoever has no money goes to Mack for credit, and who has money entrusts it to him; for banks are distant and mysterious institutions, Mack is real and near. His business is in fact built on the small sums thus put at his disposal, but he never deviates from his attitude of conferring a favor upon the lender. His self-possession, his elegance of dress, his polish of manner are unfailing. There are ugly pages in Mack's history, ruined homes, and neglected children who have the blood of the Macks in their veins, but it is part of the man's mastery that, although every member of his household knows of his orgies, he can yet command respect— and Ellen the chambermaid loves him. The description of Mack's erotic adventures, in spite of the humor Hamsun lavishes on the subject, occupies an uncomfortably large amount of space in these books, but they serve the author's purpose of throwing into relief the power of the man who, in spite of everything, remained a ruler by divine right. When his scandals became too rampant, his daughter Edvarda, then in one of her religious moods, attempted to remove the cause of offense and stirred up a revolt among her father's trusted people. Mack went to bed and simulated illness, but the confusion resulting from the absence of his directing hand was such that everybody was glad to restore the old order and have Mack at his desk again.

Hamsun likes to portray the patrician type to which Mack belonged by inherited instincts, but he also enjoys seeking out those tough-fibred people who are not descendants but become ancestors. Among them Mack's partner Benoni occupies the first place. Hamsun's playfulness has never been more delightful than when he traces the evolution of Post-Benoni, who carries the King's mail, to Benoni Hartvigsen and B. Hartvigsen, then to B. Hartwich, the partner of Mack and the husband of the great man's niece, Rosa. A big hairy creature, full of physical vim, strutting and vainglorious, wearing two coats to church in summer to show that he can afford it, boasting of his house and his furnishings patterned on Mack's, Benoni is with all his absurdities sound at the core. He has a childlike goodness and freshness that seems drawn from some unspoiled well of humanity. Benoni has his reverses. Occasionally his divinity and patron Mack finds it necessary to thrust him back into the nothingness from which he has drawn him, and people begin to call him plain Benoni again. Then his strutting waxes feeble for a while, but he soon rebounds and rises higher than before. It is almost unfair that his fallen fortunes are repaired by the ridiculous transaction of selling a mineral mountain to a mad Englishman for a fabulous sum; we feel that Benoni is quite capable of retrieving his losses by his own efforts; but this is a part of the melodramatic strain which belongs to Nordland, the country of sudden fortunes. When, in the last chapter of "Rosa," the young wife, in the dignity of her first motherhood, gently takes the reins of the household, we feel that Benoni in the future will prance with spirit, but with discretion too. Benoni and Rosa with the "prince" in the cradle are firmly rooted in their environs and have the power of growth. In such people Hamsun sees the future. They are the human stuff that endures.

In contrast to Benoni we have Rosa's first husband Nikolai Arentsen. He too is of humble birth, but while Benoni stays in the place where he has vital contacts, Nikolai pushes himself into a class where he will never be assimilated. Benoni applies his naturally good brain to wrestling with the problems near at hand, those of the fish and the sea. He is engaged in the productive work of helping to haul in the harvest of the deep. Nikolai learns a great many things by rote. He studies law and

77

comes home to practise in his native place. At first he does a thriving business on the easily stimulated mutual distrust of primitive people, but when they learn that it costs more to go to law than to make up their quarrels, their distrust is turned on the lawyer. His income soon dwindles to nothing, and the small world in which he has really no necessary function goes on without him. He has entered one of the professions that Hamsun calls sterile.

Hamsun frequently contrasts two brothers one of whom has stayed close to the soil while the other has tried to work his way into a supposedly higher sphere. In "Segelfoss City," there is L. Lassen who is unmade from a good fisherman and not completed to a bishop, while his brother Julius who has stayed in his natural environment and become a shrewd hotel-keeper has at least some contact with the realities. In "Growth of the Soil" Sivert on the farm is contrasted with Eleseus in the office, and always to the advantage of the former. In "Women at the Pump" there is a similar pair of brothers. Abel, the younger, a sweet-tempered, sturdy urchin with a natural pride in killing snakes, has had to shift for himself and make his own decisions almost from the day he left the cradle, and has developed into a fine young man. When the time is ripe, he slips naturally into the place in the community where he belongs, as the helper of an old blacksmith who needs a pair of young arms and a bright young face in the smithy. Within a short time Abel is the mainstay of the family. Frank, the elder, has been put through school and has learned a number of languages which, whether living or dead, will always remain dead to him. He is one of the children who are being "prepared for farming, fishing, cattle-raising, trade, industry, family life, dreams and religious worship" by learning

78

"the number of square miles in Switzerland and the dates of the Punic wars" and similarly vital facts. He "knew nothing of red outbursts, he never rose to the skies or fell down again, never went to the bottom or floated up. He never exposed himself to anything and had nothing to avoid. Instead of getting out of a scrape, he never got into one. Cleverly done, meagrely done. God had prepared him for a philologist."

It seems curious that Hamsun the poet should never have reminded Hamsun the sociologist that dreams have an intrinsic value, that the aspirations which carried Frank and Eleseus and the future Bishop Lassen out from their homes were in themselves a moral asset inasmuch as they stimulated not only those who went out but also those who stayed behind and had their horizons opened by contact with the outside world. It is almost as though he denounced the circulation of blood between the country and the city as bad in itself. The reason is, of course, that he has in mind certain standards and valuations which he combats as wrong and false. He ridicules the self-delusion of those who imagine they are educated because they have learned a number of things which they can repeat from books, and who suppose that "culture" consists in certain inherited or acquired customs that have nothing to do either with beauty or distinction, but are simply an absence of the marked, the characteristic, the splendid, or the primitive,—all that which is neither high nor low, but everlastingly on the same dull grey level of respectability. He derides those "whose hands are so sick that they can do nothing but form letters" and who think there is something superior about that "slave's work" writing. "It is finer to write and read than to do something with your hands, says the upper class. The lower class listens. My son shall not till the earth from which everything that crawls subsists; let him live on other people's work, says the upper class. And the lower class listens. Then one day the roar awoke, the roar of the masses. The masses have themselves learned the arts of the upper class; they can read and write. Bring here all the good things of the earth, they are ours!"

In "The Last Joy" Hamsun discusses modern education as it affects women. Ingeborg Torsen has been put through the mill of normal school together with a class of girls, some richer, some poorer than herself, but all intent on graduation and a position where they can put other girls through the same mill. She was educated away from the simple, healthy life of her mother and became a teacher without interest in her work, while her thwarted longing for marriage and motherhood became perverted into morbid desire. In his estimate of the so-called advancement of woman Hamsun reaches some of the same conclusions as Ellen Key, but in his preoccupation with the physical side of sex he fails to see what Ellen Key always insists on, that motherhood consists not only in bearing but in rearing, and that teaching is a profession which more than any other gives women who are not mothers an outlet for the moral qualities of motherhood. He fails to remember also that women as well as men may burn with the pure fire of a thirst for knowledge. Nevertheless, as a satire of a certain phase in the woman movement, when any other work was considered superior to that of the home, Hamsun's attack contains a kernel of bitter truth.

As the only real aristocracy Hamsun sees the big landed proprietors who ruled over their little world as kings. He does not idealize the origin of the great families, but thinks that from pride and will power an aristocracy may develop, provided there is money. "But it must be wealth, not pennies. Pennies are only to coddle the race and protect it from wet feet." In "Children of the Age" (1913), and its big two-volume sequel "Segelfoss City" (1915) we follow the decline of a big family who once owned all the land that Segelfoss city was standing on. The first Willatz Holmsen was a lackey who acquired money somehow and built a palace. The second Willatz Holmsen acquired culture. He added white columns to the palace and filled it with books and works of art. With him the rapid economic rise of the family reached its height. The third acquired personal distinction and a sense of noblesse oblige which his failing fortune could not support. The lieutenant, as he is called, whose life we follow in "Children of the Age," is a proud, lonely figure, unable to confide to any one that a Willatz Holmsen might not be able to do all that was expected of him, and mortgaging his house rather than disappoint any one who looked to him for funds. The fourth is a musician. He is an aristocrat in his personal habits and in his sense of obligation, but he has lost his father's gift of command because he has no longer the old faith in the divine right of his family to rule. He can knock down an impudent workman, but he can not quell by his mere presence as his father could. Democracy has seeped into his tissues. He still flings gifts about in a lavish way as the Holmsens have always done, but he avoids occasions where he would hold the centre of the stage, and is at the same time a little hurt that he is not a wonder and a fairy-tale to the people as his father and mother were. He has the modern self-doubting habit of mind, and is glad to resign the position of leadership to the new man, the captain of industry,

Holmengraa. Willatz Holmsen the fourth is, both in his fine, generous personal character and in his real genius as a musician, an illustration of Hamsun's theory that wealth in several generations will produce culture of heart and mind, but the young man's development carries him inevitably away from Segelfoss, and the brilliant career which is foreshadowed for him falls outside the frame of the story. As village potentates the Holmsens have had their day. Their dynasty is ended.

"King Tobias," as Holmengraa is called, appears in a golden cloud of romance. He is a peasant's son who has acquired a fortune in South America and comes back to his native place, turning the sleepy little village into a small city overnight. His ships bring grain from the Baltic; his mills grind day and night; he cuts timber; he establishes a telegraph station, and has work and money for everybody. But Holmengraa comes in contact with a new power which he is not strong enough to resist, that of the rising proletariat. His men read the "Segelfoss Times"which tells them that all the world rests on their toil, that they are wage slaves, and their employer is an extortioner. They make larger and larger demands; they become insolent and scoff at King Tobias who has now sunk to be plain Tobias to them. Unfortunately Holmengraa, who is a modest, fine-fibred man and very sympathetically drawn, has his weakness. Like the great Mack, he is unable to leave the girls alone, but he has not Mack's brazen assurance, and his position is gradually undermined. It is found that his fortune is not so great as first supposed, and his day is short.

So village dynasties rise and fall. At last comes one that is not too fine-grained or sensitive. Theodor Jensen with the sobriquet "paa

Bua" (in the store) is a selfmade man like Benoni, apparently slighter and frothier, more of a parody, but in reality possessed of a harder and more slippery cleverness than that of the expansive Benoni. Theodor rises out of the most malodorous surroundings, but, like Benoni, is himself sound, on the whole. The village laughs at his airs, his rings, his scarf pin made of a gold coin, his absurd pretensions; but little Theodor has what the former dynasties lacked, a faculty for meeting every situation as it arises. He has pluck and shrewdness and is not entirely lacking in generosity. He builds a big store, and all the affairs of the village revolve about him. He extends credit, and servant girls are divided into two classes, those who have credit at Theodor's and those who have not. He brings the world to Segelfoss: silk dresses, canned goods, store shoes, fireworks, a theatrical troupe—everything that can be named. In a year of depression, when everybody was in a funereal frame of mind, Theodor bethought himself of tomb-stones, and presently the graveyard blossomed out with a sudden forest of slabs and crosses with "Rest in Peace" and "Loved and Missed" on graves that had been neglected for a quarter of a century. Theodor knows what the people want. The future is his.

Hamsun has a kindness for this merry privateer and enjoys blowing the wind that swells little Theodor's sails, but underneath the froth and sparkle there is a bitter didactic purpose in this book. It shows the reverse side of modern progress, when a backward community learns to use the material conveniences of the age without any corresponding mental advancement. The workingmen have learned to make demands, but while they refuse to yield the old submission to authority, they have not learned any sense of responsibility to their own conscience, and therefore grow more and more lazy and inefficient. The women forget to cook and sew while they buy flimsy readymade clothes at the store and feed their families on food that is bought ready cooked and chewed and almost digested. Neither men nor women know what to do with their leisure, and general demoralization is the result.

"Segelfoss City," with its dying aristocracy, its captain of industry, and its spoiled working class, is a miniature mirror of the modern world as Hamsun sees it. In the same category belongs his last book, "Women at the Pump" (1920), but there the deterioration is more complete. The events recorded are only a grey dribble from a leaky town pump. "People in big cities have no idea of standards and dimensions in the small towns," so runs the opening paragraph. "They think they can come and stand in the market-place and smile and be superior. They think they can laugh at the houses and the pavements, indeed they often think so. But do not old people remember the time when the houses were still smaller and the pavements still worse? And there at least C. A. Johnson has built himself a tremendously big house, a perfect mansion. It has a veranda below and a balcony above and scroll work all the way around the roof.... The small town too has its great men, its solid families with their fine sons and daughters, its immutableness and authority. And the small world is absorbed in its great men and follows their career with interest. The good small town folk are really acting to their own advantage in doing this; they live in the shelter of authority, and it is good for them."

What indeed would the little town have been without Consul

Johnson? What glory would there have been in life without his silk hat and his rotund face beaming on the crowds as they make way respectfully? When the story opens, the village is assembled to watch the departure of his steamer, the Fia, for foreign waters. While they wait, the women at the village pump, standing with buckets filled and hands under their aprons, are discussing a great event that happened six or seven years ago, but is still undimmed in memories not over-burdened with weighty affairs. It was the day when "Johnson on the Dock" was made consul, and everybody who came into his store was treated with sweet cakes and a drink. Since then other consuls had sprung up like mushrooms; there was "Barley-Olsen" and Henriksen at the Works, but Consul Johnson's glory outshone that of all others, and his scandals only gave an added nimbus to his name. The measure of difference between Hamsun's earlier books and "Women at the Pump" may be seen in the distance between the really magnificent reprobate Mack and the flabby Consul Johnson, a man who has become a village magnate by the accident of owning the only store in the neighborhood. But village dynasties rise and fall, and the Johnson dynasty seems tottering, when it is saved by the consul's young, aggressive, thoroughly modern son, Schelderup, who suddenly comes home and raises the house of Johnson to its old glory. The consul's day is over, however, and it is pathetic to see him shrink back into the obscurity from which accident had drawn him. In his fall he appeals to us as never before, and Hamsun makes us feel that the foolish old man is, in his innermost nature, better than the hard-headed son.

Schelderup brought order into his father's affairs, but into some he brought disorder. He stopped various pensions that were being paid for reasons known to Consul Johnson and sometimes to the women at the pump. Among other drastic steps, he abolished the sinecure at the Johnson warehouse held by the cripple Oliver, and the annual subsidy paid to Oliver's son, the philologist Frank. It is Oliver who is the "hero" of the book; in him "the little town sees itself realized."

Oliver was once a sailor with powerful arms, a dashing young blade with a pretty sweetheart and his life before him. He goes away on Consul Johnson's Fia and comes back a wreck. He has lost a leg and has sustained another injury not yet the property of the village gossips: he is unable to become a father. Oliver comes home to take up his life on shore, to fish a little, to lie and cheat his way through life, to starve sometimes, to "find" sometimes the property of others, to marry his old sweetheart Petra as a screen for another man, none less in fact than the great Consul Johnson himself, and to buy back his mortgaged home as the price of her favors to another great man of the village, the member of parliament and future cabinet minister Fredriksen. He lives on the memories of the days when he went to sea and on two events that have happened to him since his return. He has once won a tablecloth in a lottery, and he has once found a derelict ship and sailed it in, a deed which resulted in putting his name in the paper.

There is only one bright spot in the life of this human wreck, who grows physically more repulsive as the years go on. Only one thing unites him in a sweet and natural relation with our common humanity, and that is his love for the children who are not his. Hamsun here takes up an interesting psychological question and arrives at the opposite conclusion from that of Strindberg in "The Father."

He shows that fatherly affection is not a primitive instinct but a growth of habit. Oliver cares for his wife's children while they are small, and when they grow up they love him and have no interest in attaching themselves to their actual fathers. Indeed Oliver's importance in the community grows in the reflected light from his successful children, although the truth about their origin has long since leaked out at the town pump. There is, of course, irony in this, but there is also a certain optimism. In his great novels picturing the life of whole communities, Hamsun has thrown the glamour of his art over a big gallery of insignificant people. Mere puppets for his amusement they seem at first, and yet, as we penetrate more deeply into his work, we feel behind the smile a great sweetness, a broad humanity, and at bottom a faith that life fashions its own ends out of all this human dross and fashions not badly.

Hamsun's social theories will be sufficiently evident from the above recapitulation of the novels in which he is holding up the mirror to his generation. He rebels against all that would cripple individual effort and against all modern standardizing whether it applies to the choice of a profession or to the cut of a garment. The levelling process which, inasmuch as it can not make all great, must achieve equality by making all small, he believes to be a disadvantage for the small, who thus lose an ideal and an element of romance in their lives. He abjures all modern shams and artificiality and particularly the false standard that exalts the white collar job above the work involving a little honest grime. He would like to see his people a nation of farmers and fishermen with an aristocracy of big landed proprietors and brainy business men, but with all the middle class of administrators and clerical workers eliminated.

With the latter he would sweep away most professional men and those who hang on the fringes of art and literature. The real genius, the poet by the grace of God, he regards as above and outside of all classes.

These theories, to which Hamsun lends the point of his whimsical, paradoxical extravagance, must be seen against a background of special conditions in a small country with a large number of brain workers proportionally, and with, perhaps, a tendency to over-value what passes for culture. Stated coldly and in detail they are, of course, impracticable. No nation or group of people can detach itself from the complications of modern civilization. Hamsun the sociologist is not on a par with Hamsun the poet. But when he leads us back to the deep, primeval well-springs without which our civilization must wither and die, it is Hamsun the poet who speaks.

GROWTH OF THE SOIL

In "Growth of the Soil" Hamsun has concentrated the message which, in more or less fragmentary form lies scattered through his works: that everything else is small compared with the one essential thing, to be in unison with nature and to work with nature in "a great friendliness." There he preaches with massive reiteration that the salvation of the modern world lies in getting back to the land, and by his poetic treatment he has linked the doctrine with the fight men have waged since the beginning of human life on earth.

Without the artifice of distant time and place, in the midst of modern conditions painted with realism and often with humor, he has created an illusion of the primeval. It is as though Isak, the man without a surname, coming we know not whence, walking through the forest in search of a place where he can begin to till the soil, were the first man in a newly created world. "There goes a path through the forest. Who made it? The man, the human being, the first one who came." He walks all day over the moors in the great stillness, turning the sod occasionally to examine its possibilities, then walks again until night comes.

Then he sleeps a while with his head on his arm, and walks again until he finds the right place for himself, and there he makes his first home on a bed of pine needles under a projecting rock.

After this prelude, which has a cadence like the first chapter of Genesis, Hamsun allows us to follow the story of how the shelter under a rock became a farm. There were no banks for lending money to pioneer farmers and no societies for the reclamation of waste land, or if there were, Isak knew nothing about them. He was only one man who met nature alone. After a while a woman came to him out of nowhere and did not leave him again. Inger was hare-lipped, and Isak with his fierce beard and grotesque strength looked like a troll of the forest; for Hamsun has scorned to throw even the glamour of youth and rustic beauty over the pair. They were simply man and woman, brought together by the most elemental needs, working together, helping each other, meeting the demands of each day as they arose, and resting when night fell. The picture of their early days together, their delight in each other and their surprise at all the wonders that happen to them, is full of innocent, primitive charm.

There is an idyllic beauty about the first chapters of the book, but "Growth of the Soil" is not primarily an idyl. It is the story of human achievement centering in Isak's intense, never-ceasing effort to subdue the small part of the earth which he has taken for his own. It is almost as though he were really the first man without the accumulated resources of civilization behind him. He sleeps under the rock until he has completed a sod hut which gives him shelter against the cold and rain, and by and by a window is added to let in the daylight. In the course of time the sod hut gives place to a real house of logs, and the sod hut can be left to the animals.

One day Inger disappears leaving Isak feeling very lost and lonely, but presently she comes back leading a cow, an event so great and wonderful that they spend their first wakeful night discussing it. Isak can hardly believe that the cow is theirs, but he makes the retort courteous by bringing a horse for his contribution. As for goats and sheep, they are already a little herd. The meadows yield grass, the grain ripens for harvest. Everything grows and thrives, grain, animals, human beings. There is a fruitfulness, a teeming, a bringing forth of everything that lives on the earth and by the earth. It is like looking on at a bit of the creation of the world. And there are Biblical parallels too with the man who came across the moor with a bag of bread and cheese and became the patriarch of a countryside.

Isak's strong, unused brain is developed by the necessity for helping himself. He invents various clever contrivances. He learns how to plan his work and fit one task into another so that every month of the year is utilized to the utmost advantage. He sows and reaps and mows; he threshes the grain on a threshing-floor of his own construction and grinds it in a mill which he has also made. He fells and trims the logs for his house, cuts them in a saw-mill which he has made with infinite effort and cogitation, and fits them together in the expert fashion which he has learned by studying the methods used in the village. The foundation has been laid of stones from his own land, lifted with his own brawny strength. An especially huge stone or an unusually big piece of timber put in its place is to him as real a triumph as the honors and emoluments of the world are to the more sophisticated. Isak revels in his work, and his powers grow with his tasks. He is a happy man.

The contrast between Isak's absorption in his work and the lazy, discontented apathy of the industrial laborers in "Segelfoss City" is, of course, evident. In the same manner the upbringing of his boys is contrasted with the education of children who are put through the usual school routine. While the latter are mere passive recipients of a knowledge which is thrust upon them from the outside without regard to their needs, the boys in the wilderness are allowed to develop naturally and from within. Every bit of knowledge that they acquire comes in response to the necessity for meeting a practical situation. They are stimulated by their father's example, as they are allowed to help him, and they exert their small brains to give the right answer when he asks their advice in all seriousness. Hamsun here returns to the subject of the transplanted country boy which has engaged his interest from the publication of "Shallow Soil," and allows the elder of Isak's boys, Eleseus, to attract the interest of a visitor who takes him to town and puts him in an office. The result is that the boy wilts like an uprooted plant. He is not bad, he is simply futile. He has lost interest in country pursuits without having any marked ability that would insure him a career in the city, and he has been imbued with the idea that it would be a step downward for him to go back from his poorly paid office job to the work of the farm. When he comes home, he tries hard to please his father, for he is a good, affectionate lad, but he has lost the poise of those who have stayed on the land. He has been infected by the restlessness of those who have no resources in themselves, but are for ever running about to have

92

their emptiness filled by the drippings from other people's lives—from newspapers, moving pictures, street corner gossip. Sivert, the younger brother, stays at home, and it is he who continues to build on the foundation laid by the father.

The people in the wilderness have not had their minds made a sieve for the happenings of the outside world and have not inhaled the mental atmosphere that has been breathed again and again by millions of people. Their imaginations are fresh and strong, and they have time to live to the full in whatever happens to them. From every experience they draw the utmost that it contains of joy or sorrow. There is stillness and breadth of vision. Everything has its appointed place, and though human beings in their flightiness may stray from their orbit, the great forces that dwell in nature draw them back and hold them.

There is bigness and simplicity in their joys and sorrows and even in their sins. When Inger kills her hare-lipped baby to save it from the suffering she has endured because of the blemish in her own face, the story of how she buries the little body in the baptismal robe of her firstborn and puts a cross on the grave is profoundly touching. Her real grief and repentance, her meek submission to punishment and her thankfulness that her life is spared, Isak's grief and unfailing love, his loneliness and longing for her return from prison, all these belong to people who meet life without evasion or subterfuge.

While Inger's crime is raised to the level of tragedy, the story of the girl Barbro who kills her two children in pure wantonness and is acquitted in the new "humane" spirit after a parody of a trial, is a hideous, sordid tale. Hamsun here contrasts the people who live among the great realities, accepting the consequences of their deeds, with those who have learned to play tricks with life and cheat the Goddess of Justice. This to a certain extent justifies the inclusion of Barbro's story in the book, although it mars the big epic lines of the rest by its rather journalistic attacks on criminal procedure and satire of a certain type of "advanced" woman who espouses Barbro's cause. It was, as a matter of fact, an outgrowth of some polemical articles with the keynote "Hang them!" which Hamsun wrote in the Norwegian press, when the growing slackness in the treatment of women indicted for child murder had roused his indignation. Ugly as the story is, it ends on the note of optimism which runs like a golden vein through "Growth of the Soil." There is a hint that Barbro and her lover, the hard, grasping farmer, as they marry and settle down to till the soil, may be reclaimed by their work in harmony with the beneficent forces of nature. There is a suggestion that nature is great enough to absorb even the vicious and take them into her service.

Isak himself, a tiller of the soil by the grace of God, is the one person in the book who never deviates from the straight course. He is immutably rooted in the eternal verities. As the story progresses, his figure grows until it assumes a certain grandeur. He draws from his humble work a deep and gentle comprehension. There is forgiveness in him and strength to raise up what life has shattered. Isak has his oddities, but they light up his character like sunbeams playing over the face of a rock. How inimitable, for instance, the story, told with Hamsun's gift of comicality without malice, of how Isak brings home a mowing-machine, the first seen in the neighborhood; of how he drives solemnly sitting on the machine in his best winter suit and hat, as befits the importance of the occasion, although the sweat is running down his face; how he swells under the admiration of his womankind, and how he pretends that he has forgotten his spectacles, because, in fact, he can make neither head or tail of the printed instructions. When fate plays him the trick of letting the spectacles slip out of his pocket, although the boys pretend they do not see it, Isak is conscious that he is perhaps being punished for his overweening pride.

Isak's superstitions always take the form of thinking that when he does what is required of him, fate will be merciful. His dim religious sense, drawing all the small things of life in under the shelter of a great fundamental rightness which rules the world and in some mysterious way takes cognizance of his affairs, reminds me of "Adam Bede." Isak never read any book except the almanac and could not formulate his thoughts on religion, but he feels God in the loneliness, under the starry heavens, and in the might of the forest. He meets God one night on the moor and does not deny that he has also met the devil, but he drives him away in Jesu name. When the children grow large enough to ask questions, he can not teach them anything out of books, and the Catechism is generally allowed to repose on the shelf with the goat cheeses, but he tells them how the stars are made and implants the dream in their hearts.

An act which has something of an almost priestly function is the sowing of grain. That newfangled fruit, the potato, could be planted by women and children, but grain, which meant bread, had to be sown by the head of the house, and Isak went about his task devoutly as his forefathers had done for hundreds of years, sowing the grain in Jesu name. Twice Hamsun repeats the description of Isak sowing, and it is like a picture by Millet. With head religiously bared, he walks in the setting sun, his great beard and bushy hair standing round him like a wheel, his limbs like gnarled trees, while the tiny grains fly from his hands in an arch and fall like a rain of gold into the ground.

It is difficult at this time to say how future generations will judge "Growth of the Soil." We are still too near the events that made it to us an epochal book. It would be easy to pick flaws, and I have already mentioned what seems to me its most serious fault, the inclusion of an arid waste of discussion on child murder and its punishment. It would be easy, too, to say that its purpose was too patent, its sermon too direct. Nevertheless, the very simplicity and bigness of this purpose make it susceptible to artistic treatment, and I think there can be no question but that Hamsun has produced a great piece of literature which will stand the test of time.

What matters, after all, is not what critics will say of its esthetic merits. The supreme importance of the book lies in the fact that to Hamsun's own generation it has given poetic form to a message for which the world was thirsting. At a time when humanity was sick of destruction he reminded us that nature's fountain of renewal is inexhaustible. In an age which has been saddened by the pernicious doctrine of competition, the survival of the fittest, and all the slogans of false Darwinism, he preached the gospel of friendliness. We have been told that nature is cruel; Hamsun says that nature is friendly and beneficent. We have been told that all existence rests on fierce competition in which the weaker must go under. He does not deny that the battle is to

96

the strong and the race to the swift; Isak does what no weaker man could have compassed, but Isak treads down no one on his way. On the contrary, his strength is the shelter under which the weaker can grow and flourish. He made the first path, but scores of people and hundreds of animals come to live in the wilderness through which he walked alone.

Competition with its fear and agony arises because people want to run faster than life. Peace and happiness are found in keeping pace with life. The modern business man is like the lightning which flashes here and there, "But lightning as lightning is sterile," says Geissler, the author's spokesman; and he speaks words of wisdom to young Sivert of Sellanraa: "Look at you Sellanraa people: every day you gaze at some blue mountains. They are not figments of the imagination, they are old mountains sunk deep in the past; and you have them for companions. You live here with heaven and earth and are one with them, you are one with all the broad and deeply-rooted things. You do not need a sword in your hands; you meet life bare-headed and bare-handed in the midst of a great friendliness. Look, there is nature, it belongs to you and to your people! Men and nature are not bombarding each other, they agree. They are not competing or running a race, they go together. In the midst of this you Sellanraa people exist. The mountains, the woods, the moors, the meadows, the heavens, and the stars—oh, nothing of this is poor and grudging, it is without measure. Listen to me, Sivert, be content! You have everything to live on, everything to live for, everything to believe in, you are born and produce, you are the necessary ones on earth. Not all are necessary on earth, but you are. You preserve life. From generation to generation you exist in nothing but fruitfulness, and when you die another generation carries it on. That is what is meant by life eternal."

THE WANDERER ARRIVED

Two tendencies war with each other in the temperament of the Norwegians. One has made them vikings, explorers, seafarers, and pioneers; the other has made them home-builders and tillers of the soil. One is restless, impatient of restraint, avid for new experiences and for ever-shifting forms of life; the other longs for the homeland, and seeks to strike roots deep in the spot of earth made sacred by the toil of the forefathers.

In Knut Hamsun both these tendencies are present and are accentuated by his double racial heritage, his birth in an old peasant family of Gudbrandsdalen and his upbringing among the lively, adventurous fisherfolk of Nordland. In his work, the two strains are evident, the former predominating in his earlier, the latter in his recent books. Glahn, the untamed hunter and nomad, is a true child of the author's spirit, but so is Isak, the farmer and home-builder. The common bond that unites them is that both are closely affiliated with nature, one as the passionate lyrical worshipper of Pan, the other as the humble servant of nature's fruitfulness.

In the personal life of the author the same divergent tendencies may be traced. He has been a wanderer on the face of the earth, a vagrant laborer in Norway, a pioneer in America, a visitor to the capitals of Europe, a traveller in the Orient. But deep inherited instincts have always drawn him homeward. He has sought a place where his own life could strike root. Since the year 1896 he has made his home in Norway, and ever since the financial returns of his early books made it possible, has lived on his own land and cultivated it. His first home was in Nordland, at Hamaröy in Salten. There he lived for many years, surrounded by the wild, majestic, yet ingratiating scenery which impressed him in boyhood and which he has so often pictured. In 1917 he removed to the south of Norway, and, after a short residence at Larvik on the Christianiafjord, chose his present home near Grimstad, the small seaport town where Ibsen spent his unhappy youth as an apothecary's apprentice. There he has bought the estate Nörholmen with a fine mansion several hundred years old.

Though Hamsun has lived as much as possible in the outskirts of human settlement and has always kept in retirement, denying himself to sightseers and above all to interviewers, the kindliness which breathes from his work and, in spite of his nervous shyness, emanates from his personality, has made him very much beloved in his own country. A very sympathetic picture of his home life is presented by the Norwegian newspaper writer, Thomas Vetlesen, who in the autumn of 1920 was admitted to Hamsun's home through the good offices of the government. As it is the only authentic account we have, I will quote here a portion of the article which appeared in the Norwegian press.

"After a half hour's drive (from Grimstad) we enter a lane of hazel nut bushes, bending over the road weighted by their full, heavy clusters of nuts. Soon we catch sight of Hamsun's white, two-story house at the end of a quiet bight of the sea, not far from the main road. The automobile swings into the large yard with a quick, accustomed motion, and stops in front of the kitchen steps. The noise has announced my arrival, and presently the yard is full of people. Fru Hamsun and the children receive the stranger and welcome him to their home. There is Tore and Arild and Elinor and the lovely little Cecilie — a pretty four-leaf clover at ages ranging from three to nine summers.

"Within the house the spacious rooms with their pleasant old-fashioned style of building breathe a spirit of hospitality. There is a garden room turning out toward the road, a dining-room, a wide hall with a staircase leading to the upper story and on the other side of it a series of smaller rooms.

"Knut Hamsun comes in quickly from the hall, straight and tall, with powerful shoulders and head unbent by time and mental labor. His handclasp is firm and warm, but in his melodious voice there is an undertone of something veiled, wistful, almost hurt, which suggests the tremendous mental strain his intensive work has subjected him to for many years past.

"At the supper table Hamsun asks about mutual friends, touches lightly on current events, but is not talkative. Occasionally he seems to remember suddenly that he is getting too taciturn. But his thoughts are in Hazel Valley where he has chosen for his work room an ancient cottage built in the wilderness for herders. There he spends the entire day outside of meal hours, surrounded by the great stillness and by what seems a chaos of small bits of white paper filled with writing. Here is his work room, here he can have peace. Woe to him who would draw near to his circles! As yet no one has ever done it with impunity. There are the wildest reports current about the more than simple appointments of this Tusculum, where he has conceived and written his books for some years past.

"After supper, when he has lit his pipe, Hamsun generally selects a chair near the sofa where he has placed his visitor, and then he unbends. Quietly and naturally, the conversation turns on many things. He can ask questions, and he can tell a story well, vividly and entertainingly, in a vein all his own. His comments are often startling, full of cut and thrust, never malicious, but instinct with kindliness and understanding. As he talks, the listener is deeply conscious of the fact that he is a good man, a sensitive nature, with a heart and a spirit open to the weal and woe of humanity. And there is music in his voice. Even when talks of everyday matters, there is about everything he says an elevation that makes what he says impressive. It is like a glimmer of northern lights, often fantastic, always fascinating and strangely compelling. His sense of humor is never far away, and his laughter has a wonderfully young note rising from his healthy lungs....

"The interest that overshadows everything else in his mind is the farm, the work on the fields, in the barn, and with the cattle. He cares little for any other position and task than that of the farmer—with the possible exception of the sailor and the aviator; he willingly admitted that the latter might have a great future.

Nothing delights him more than when he finds in his children proclivities for the work on the farm.

"It is rare to see a man so fond of children as Hamsun is. He never tires of hearing about the sayings and doings of his four fine children. He pays attention to whatever they say and studies their different aptitudes and their thoughts....

"Hamsun has a very large library containing many rare and curious books. What he likes best to read is memoirs and books of travel. In addition to his absorbing work on his new book 'Women at the Pump,' he has of late been extremely busy developing his estate Nörholmen. He has accomplished much, but much remains to be done. When in future years it is completed, it will form an interesting Hamsun chapter in itself."

While the author has been living his quiet, retired life, divided between his prodigious industry as a writer and his concern for home and farm, his fame has been spreading to the whole civilized world. In his own country he has long been acknowledged king, the greatest of living authors, the most widely read, the most beloved. In Sweden critics have acclaimed him as the most popular writer in the Scandinavian North, in spite of the fact that Sweden has among her own authors now living several stars of the first magnitude. In the autumn of 1920, Knut Hamsun received from the hand of the Swedish king the greatest formal recognition that can come to any man of letters, the Nobel Prize for literature. Outside of the Scandinavian countries he first became known in Russia, where the people regard him almost as one of their own. In Germany and Austria he has also been widely read for many years past. In France he has only recently become known, while in England and America it was the tremendous impression made by "Growth of the Soil" which drew attention to his earlier works and was the beginning of a popularity that promises to become enduring fame.